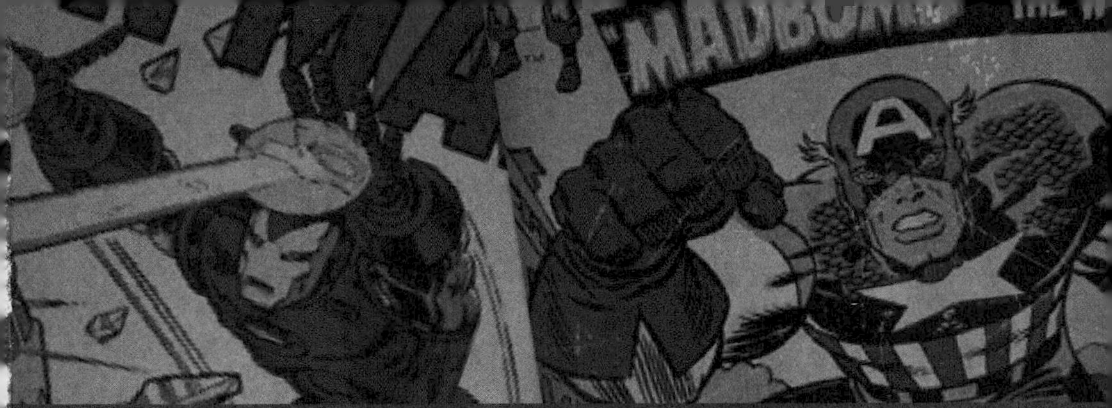

MARVEL

MY ULTIMATE SUPER HERO MANUAL

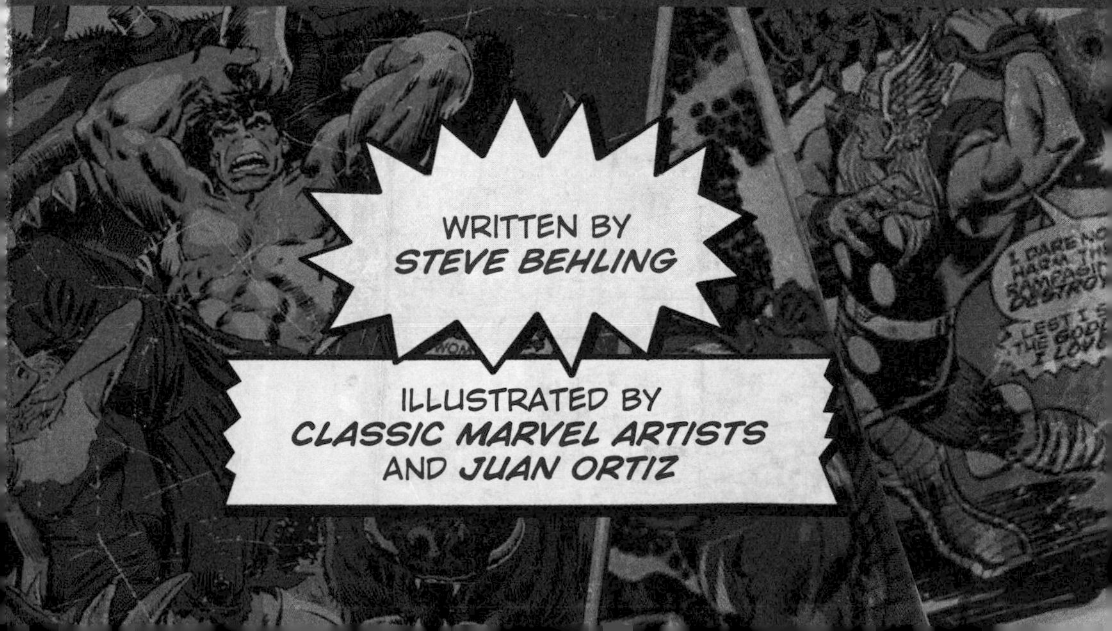

WRITTEN BY
STEVE BEHLING

ILLUSTRATED BY
CLASSIC MARVEL ARTISTS
AND *JUAN ORTIZ*

THIS BOOK BELONGS TO:

Hump man

(*WRITE* YOUR *REAL* NAME HERE, OR YOUR *SUPER HERO* NAME FOR THAT MATTER. IT'S YOUR BOOK. GO CRAZY.)

STOP!

YOU KNOW THE *KIND* OF BOOKS THAT YOUR PARENTS TELL YOU *NOT* TO WRITE IN? THE *ONES* THAT YOU CAN'T TAKE A PEN OR PENCIL TO, THAT YOU *CAN'T* DRAW IN? THE *REALLY* DUSTY BOOKS THAT *NOBODY* LOOKS AT, LIKE THAT *ONE* ABOUT *SHOES* THROUGH HISTORY?

THIS *ISN'T* THAT KIND OF BOOK.

WE *WANT* YOU TO WRITE IN IT. WE *WANT* YOU TO DRAW IN IT. YOU'LL MAKE THE HULK *ANGRY* IF YOU DON'T.*

STOP! AGAIN!

IN *THIS* BOOK, YOU'RE GOING TO *CREATE* YOUR VERY OWN *MARVEL SUPER HERO*. YOU'LL DETERMINE EVERYTHING: YOUR *NAME*, YOUR *ORIGIN*, YOUR *POWERS*, *ALLIES*, *ENEMIES*, AND *MORE*. WHEN YOU'RE ALL *DONE*, YOU'LL BE ABLE TO *PLAY* AN *ADVENTURE* WITH YOUR SUPER HERO AND *FACE* SOME OF THE MOST *SINISTER* SUPER VILLAINS IMAGINABLE. *ALSO* THE GIBBON.

*WE *DON'T* HAVE THE BUDGET TO DEAL WITH AN *ANGRY* HULK, SO.

FOR *JAMES* AND *EMMA*,
MY *SUPER HERO* AND *SUPER VILLAIN*.
YOU GUYS FIGURE OUT *WHO'S* WHO.

MARVEL
COMICS

First Edition, August 2016   10 9 8 7 6 5 4 3 2 1

ISBN 978-1-4847-5075-9

FAC-008598-16176

Library of Congress Control Number: 2015906749

Cover and interior design by Kurt Hartman

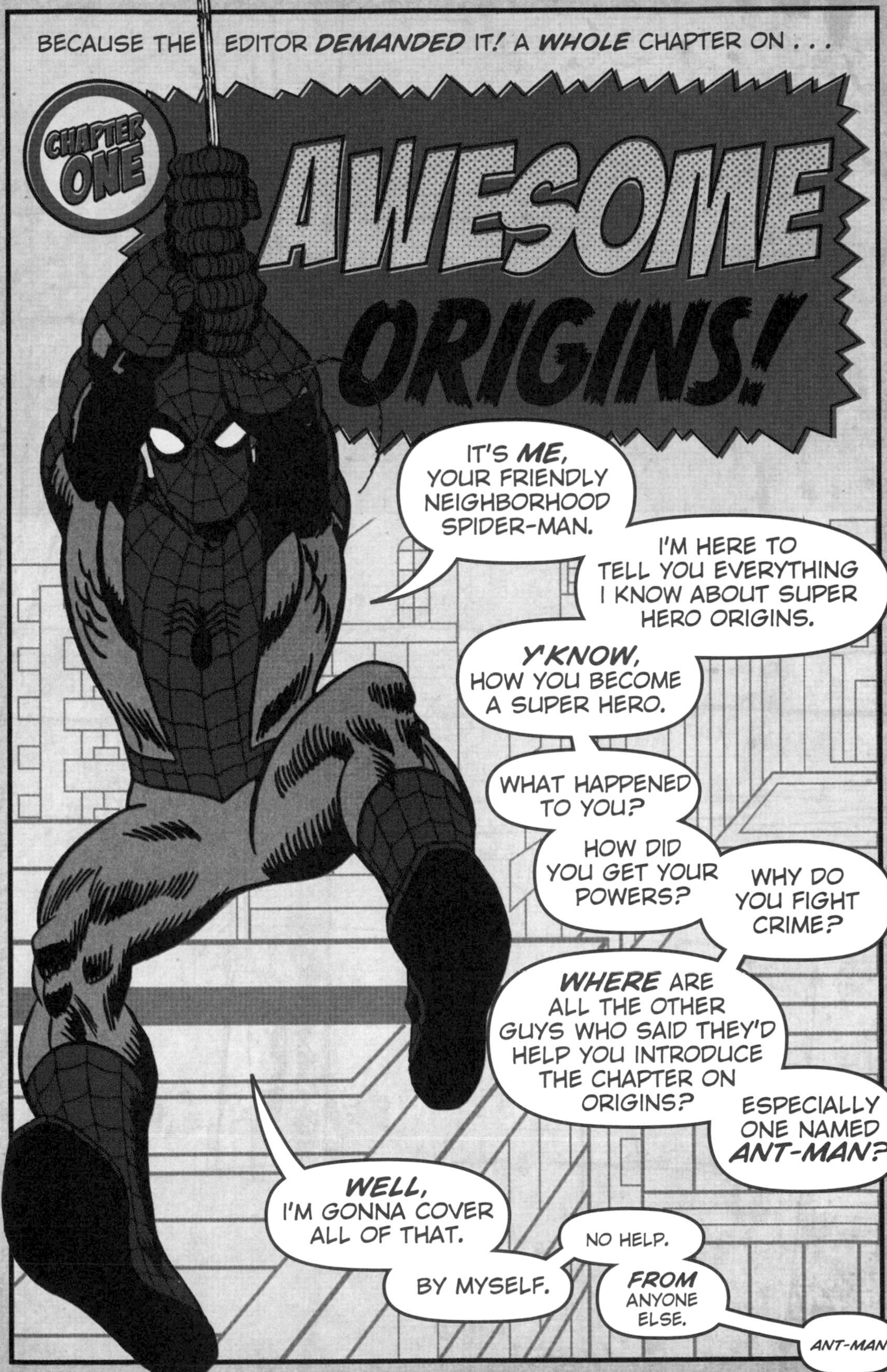
BECAUSE THE EDITOR DEMANDED IT! A WHOLE CHAPTER ON . . .
CHAPTER ONE
AWESOME ORIGINS!
IT'S ME, YOUR FRIENDLY NEIGHBORHOOD SPIDER-MAN.
I'M HERE TO TELL YOU EVERYTHING I KNOW ABOUT SUPER HERO ORIGINS.
Y'KNOW, HOW YOU BECOME A SUPER HERO.
WHAT HAPPENED TO YOU?
HOW DID YOU GET YOUR POWERS?
WHY DO YOU FIGHT CRIME?
WHERE ARE ALL THE OTHER GUYS WHO SAID THEY'D HELP YOU INTRODUCE THE CHAPTER ON ORIGINS?
ESPECIALLY ONE NAMED ANT-MAN?
WELL, I'M GONNA COVER ALL OF THAT.
BY MYSELF.
NO HELP.
FROM ANYONE ELSE.
ANT-MAN.

TWO THINGS!

In *THIS* chapter, you'll find *TWO* Marvel Universe questions you need to answer about your super hero origin. You'll write your answers on the *MARVEL UNIVERSE SHEET* provided on page 165. We'll talk *ALL* about 'em in *THIS* chapter, but here's the short version!

WHAT'S YOUR ORIGIN?

WHY DO YOU FIGHT CRIME?

AWESOME ORIGINS

High school student Peter Parker and his classmates were attending a routine demonstration on radioactivity (you know, like you do). But what happened next was anything *BUT* routine! No one noticed a *TINY* spider gliding through the radioactive rays. The dying spider *BIT* Peter, transferring all its powers to him!

Not *everyone* can be bitten by a radioactive spider *or* belted by gamma rays *or* create their own suit of super-powered armor. The law of averages says that, sooner or later, *somebody's* origin is gonna be kind of *lame*. Here are some of the *least* cool super hero origins.

LEAST COOL ORIGINS

10. Licked by radioactive camel

9. Ate entire case of canned yams

8. Born with extra belly button

7. Saw a bat

6. Injected with squid DNA

5. Found ancient gnarled cane, slammed it against rock; turned out to be just an ancient gnarled cane

4. Stole Hulk's ice cream, became Run Really Fast Man

3. Ran out of Super-Soldier Serum, given Super-Sleepy Serum instead

2. Slipped on sentient banana peel

1. Lived with kangaroos, learned how to jump just like them

WAIT . . .

THAT LAST ONE IS *MY* ORIGIN.

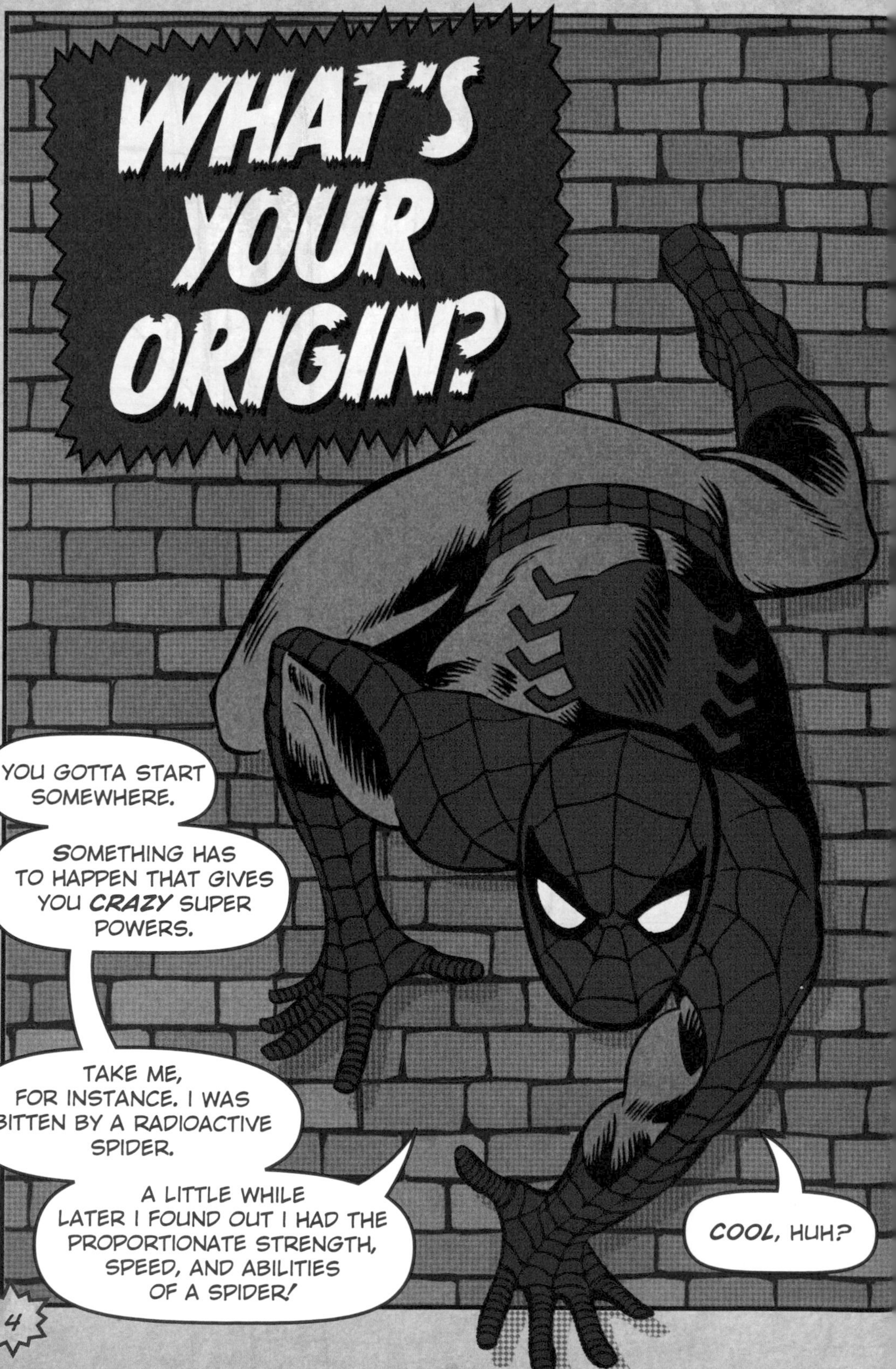
WHAT'S YOUR ORIGIN?
YOU GOTTA START SOMEWHERE.
SOMETHING HAS TO HAPPEN THAT GIVES YOU CRAZY SUPER POWERS.
TAKE ME, FOR INSTANCE. I WAS BITTEN BY A RADIOACTIVE SPIDER.
A LITTLE WHILE LATER I FOUND OUT I HAD THE PROPORTIONATE STRENGTH, SPEED, AND ABILITIES OF A SPIDER!
COOL, HUH?

WHETHER IT'S AN ACCIDENT, A TOP-SECRET EXPERIMENT, OR AN INVENTION OF YOUR VERY OWN, YOU NEED TO FIGURE OUT HOW YOU GET YOUR POWERS. LUCKY FOR YOU, WE'VE GOT IT COVERED! ALL YOU HAVE TO DO IS PICK ONE THING FROM *COLUMN A* AND ONE THING FROM COLUMN *B*. THEN WRITE YOUR ANSWER IN THE *ORIGIN* SPACE ON YOUR *MARVEL UNIVERSE* SHEET ON PAGE 166.

PSSST!

USE THE BLANK SPACES BELOW TO WRITE IN YOUR OWN IDEAS!

SECRET ORIGIN CHECKLIST

COLUMN A

☐ Bitten by

☐ Abducted by

☐ Trained by

☐ Zapped by

☐ Bestowed by

☐ Trampled by

☐ _____

☐ _____

☐ _____

☐ _____

COLUMN B

☐ a radioactive gopher

☐ lazy aliens

☐ a master chef

☐ an unstable molecule ray

☐ The Norse god of belching

☐ a hybrid cheetah-bull

☐ _____

☐ _____

☐ _____

☐ _____

SECRET ORIGIN: _____

MAKE YOUR OWN ORIGIN!

YOU'VE JUST BEEN SENT A MYSTERIOUS LETTER. *WHEN* YOU PICK UP THE PAPER, YOU NOTICE SOMETHING ALL OVER IT. YOU FEEL STRANGE–*DIFFERENT!* YOU FIND YOURSELF BATHED IN AN EERIE PURPLE LIGHT. GLANCING DOWN, YOU SEE THAT YOUR HANDS . . . *ARE GLOWING!* WHAT STRANGE SUBSTANCE HAVE YOU BEEN EXPOSED TO . . . AND WHAT POWERS WILL YOU GET?

THOUGH *I* AM *FORBIDDEN* TO INTERFERE . . .

YOU MAY ASK A PARENT OR GUARDIAN FOR HELP!

WHAT YOU'LL NEED

- Petroleum jelly
- Black-light flashlight or bulb
- Piece of paper
- Laboratory setting (optional)

THE SETUP

SPREAD SOME OF THE PETROLEUM JELLY ON A PIECE OF PAPER.

TURN ON THE BLACK-LIGHT FLASHLIGHT, AND PUT IT IN A BATHROOM. TURN OUT THE OTHER LIGHTS.

CLICK

ON

OFF

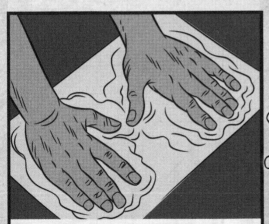

PUT THE PALMS OF BOTH HANDS ON THE PETROLEUM-JELLY PAPER. MAKE SURE THEY'RE GOOD AND COVERED!

GO INTO THE BATHROOM. WHEN YOU LOOK AT YOUR HANDS IN THE BLACK LIGHT, THEY'LL APPEAR TO GLOW!

FIN

AWESOME ORIGINS

I'VE DISARMED HIM--AND I CAN FINISH IT!

IMAGINE TEENAGE KAMALA KHAN'S *SHOCK* WHEN SHE DISCOVERED ONE DAY THAT SHE HAD *SUPER POWERS!* KAMALA IS AN *INHUMAN*—A MEMBER OF A RACE OF GENETICALLY MODIFIED HUMANS! WHEN SHE WAS EXPOSED TO THE *TERRIGEN* MIST, A CHEMICAL MADE FROM RARE CRYSTALS, KAMALA GAINED UNBELIEVABLE SHAPE-CHANGING ABILITIES. INSPIRED BY HER FAVORITE SUPER HERO, *CAPTAIN MARVEL*, KHAN CALLED HERSELF *MS. MARVEL* AND DEVOTED HER LIFE TO HELPING OTHERS.

INCREDIBLE INSPIRATION!

JUST AS *MS. MARVEL* WAS INSPIRED BY HER IDOL, *CAPTAIN MARVEL*, YOU CAN TAKE INSPIRATION FROM YOUR FAVORITE SUPER HEROES! *WHAT* DO THE HEROES DO THAT MAKES YOU WANT TO BE A BETTER PERSON? *IS* THERE SOMETHING SUPER COOL ABOUT THE WAY A HERO FAKES OUT THE FORCES OF EVIL? *THINK* ABOUT YOUR FAVORITE GOOD GUYS, AND USE THE SPACE BELOW TO WRITE IN THREE THINGS THAT *INSPIRE* YOU TO BE A *SUPER HERO.*

_____

_____

_____

NAME GAME

You can use this handy random-real-name generator to pick your name! *JUST* use the number dice to *PICK* your *FIRST NAME* (you get two options for each number). Then *ROLL AGAIN* for your *LAST NAME*. It's easy as pie! *MMMM*, pie.

1	FRANK / FRANCINE	FAULKNER
2	VICTOR / VICTORIA	VENTURA
3	JACKSON / JACQUELINE	JENKINS
4	QUINCY / QUINN	QADIR
5	WELLINGTON / WINONA	WEATHERLY
6	GUSTAV / GUINEVERE	GUNKELMAN

YOU NOTICE HOW *A LOT* OF HEROES HAVE FIRST NAMES AND LAST NAMES THAT BEGIN WITH THE *SAME* LETTER?

LIKE *PETER PARKER* . . .

BRUCE BANNER . . .

STEPHEN STRANGE . . . ?

9

PEOPLE ARE **CONSTANTLY** GETTING SUPER POWERS. IT'S A FACT OF LIFE IN THE **MARVEL UNIVERSE**. EVEN THE SIMPLE ACT OF GOING HOME HAS THE POTENTIAL TO BECOME AN ORIGIN **MOMENT!** DON'T BELIEVE US? JUST TRY TO MAKE IT FROM THE **DAILY BUGLE** BUILDING TO YOUR APARTMENT WITHOUT RUNNING INTO SOME **NUTTY** ACCIDENT THAT GIVES YOU SUPER POWERS.

A-MAZE-ING ORIGINS!

START

RADIOACTIVE PIANO

SPARE SUIT OF IRON MAN ARMOR

SWARM OF FLYING FISH

GUM TRUCK

INTERDIMENSIONAL PORTAL

END?

BUT YOU'LL *HAVE* TO DO IT AGAIN TOMORROW!

11

WHEN TONY STARK WAS **CAPTURED** BY TERRORISTS, HE WAS FORCED TO CREATE A WEAPON FOR THEM. HE BUILT IT, BUT UNFORTUNATELY FOR HIS CAPTORS, STARK DIDN'T GIVE IT TO THEM! **INSTEAD**, HE DONNED THE SUIT OF ARMOR HE HAD BUILT AND USED IT TO ESCAPE. **SINCE** THEN, STARK HAS DEVOTED HIS LIFE TO MAKING THE WORLD A **SAFER** PLACE AS THE **INVINCIBLE IRON MAN**.

MAKE YOUR OWN SUIT OF ARMOR!

YOU'D BE SURPRISED HOW EASY IT IS TO MAKE YOUR OWN SUIT OF HIGH-TECH SUPER HERO ARMOR. AND BY "**EASY**," WE MEAN, "IT WILL NEVER, **EVER** HAPPEN." WITHOUT TONY STARK'S **IQ** AND MAD ARMOR-BUILDING SKILLS, YOU'LL NEED TO FOLLOW THESE SIMPLE* STEPS TO GET A SUIT LIKE IRON MAN'S.

STEP 1: GET A JOB THAT PAYS GOOD MONEY. **LOTS** OF MONEY. LIKE, **ALL** THE MONEY. SUITS OF POWERED ARMOR ARE **NOT** CHEAP.

STEP 2: USE **ALL** THE MONEY TO HIRE TONY STARK TO MAKE YOU A SUIT OF ARMOR.

STEP 3: FIGHT CRIME!

*NOT SIMPLE

WHAT DO YOU DO ALL DAY?

EVEN SUPER HEROES NEED *TO EAT*, WHICH MEANS YOU *NEED* A JOB TO EARN MONEY TO BUY FOOD LIKE PIZZA, WHICH IS UNIVERSALLY ACKNOWLEDGED AS PRETTY MUCH THE *BEST* FOOD *EVER. NOPE*, PIZZA DOES NOT GROW ON TREES, AND JOBS DON'T, EITHER.

YOU KNOW WHAT *I* DO ALL DAY?

PRETTY MUCH *DREAD* ANYTHING THAT LOOKS LIKE HOMEWORK.

THIS LOOKS LIKE HOMEWORK.

PICK THE AREA OF YOUR EXPERTISE BY ROLLING THE *NUMBER DICE*. THEN WRITE YOUR CHARACTER'S JOB IN THE OCCUPATION SPACE ON THE *MARVEL UNIVERSE* SHEET.

1	**GAME DESIGNER**
2	**FISH TRAINER**
3	**ASTRONAUT**
4	**SCIENTIST**
5	**LIBRARIAN**
6	**PIZZA CHEF** *(which is universally acknowledged as pretty much the best job ever)*

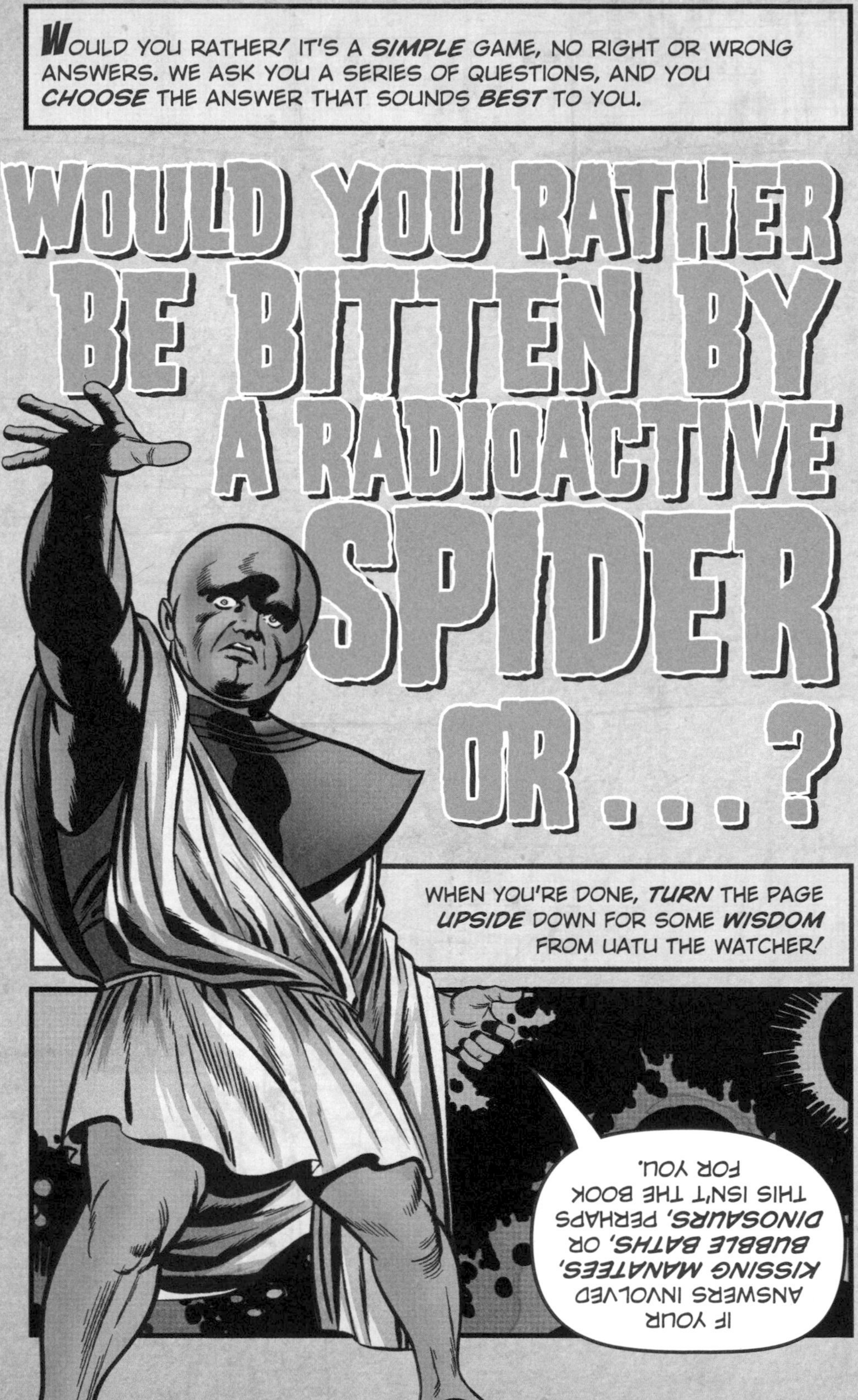
WOULD YOU RATHER! IT'S A SIMPLE GAME, NO RIGHT OR WRONG ANSWERS. WE ASK YOU A SERIES OF QUESTIONS, AND YOU CHOOSE THE ANSWER THAT SOUNDS BEST TO YOU.
WOULD YOU RATHER BE BITTEN BY A RADIOACTIVE SPIDER OR . . . ?
WHEN YOU'RE DONE, TURN THE PAGE UPSIDE DOWN FOR SOME WISDOM FROM UATU THE WATCHER!
IF YOUR ANSWERS INVOLVED KISSING MANATEES, BUBBLE BATHS, OR DINOSAURS, PERHAPS THIS ISN'T THE BOOK FOR YOU.

WOULD YOU RATHER . . .

BE BITTEN BY A RADIOACTIVE SPIDER? OR BE KISSED BY A RADIOACTIVE MANATEE?

WOULD YOU RATHER . . .

BE BATHED IN GAMMA RAYS? OR BATHE IN A DELIGHTFUL FROTHY BUBBLE BATH?

WOULD YOU RATHER . . .

TRAIN A CHILD TO BE A SUPER SPY? OR TRAIN A DINOSAUR?

AWESOME ORIGINS

SCIENTIST BRUCE BANNER WAS EXPERIMENTING WITH VOLATILE GAMMA RAYS. AS OFTEN HAPPENS WHEN ONE IS EXPERIMENTING WITH VOLATILE GAMMA RAYS, AN ACCIDENT OCCURRED: BANNER WAS BLASTED BY AN *INTENSE* DOSE OF GAMMA RADIATION. ***NOW*** WHENEVER HE BECOMES ANGRY, HE TRANSFORMS INTO THE GREEN-SKINNED GOLIATH KNOWN AS . . .

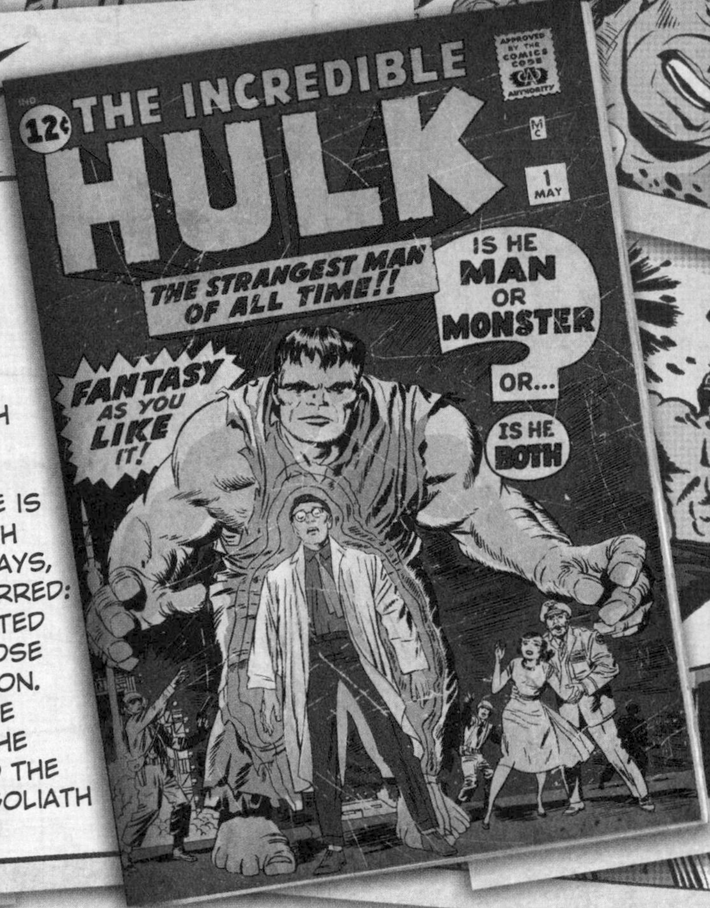

12¢
THE INCREDIBLE
HULK
APPROVED BY THE COMICS CODE AUTHORITY
MC
1 MAY
THE STRANGEST MAN OF ALL TIME!!
IS HE MAN OR MONSTER
OR...
IS HE BOTH
FANTASY AS YOU LIKE IT!

A RAY IS A RAY IS A RAY . . .

EVERYONE KNOWS THAT GAMMA RAYS WILL TURN YOU GREEN AND STRONG. BUT WHAT WILL *OTHER* RAYS TURN YOU INTO?

TYPE OF RAY	WILL TURN YOU INTO . . .
ULTRAVIOLET	*An uncomfortably sunburned human*
ALPHA	*An uncomfortably sunburned engine of destruction*
BETA	*A moody duck-billed swamp creature*
X-RAY	*Nothing cool, but lets you see pictures of your tummy*

Ferd

(Your name here)

SMASH!

WHAT YOU'LL NEED

- Water-based face paint (ask someone at your local craft store)
- A makeup sponge
- The face part of your head

THE SETUP

1. **MAKE** SURE YOU'RE WEARING AN **OLD** SHIRT SO YOUR MOM WON'T **FREAK** OUT WHEN YOU GET PAINT ON IT.

2. **DIP** THE MAKEUP SPONGE INTO THE GREEN FACE PAINT (OR ANOTHER COLOR, IF YOU PREFER).

3. SLOWLY AND CAREFULLY **DAB** THE SPONGE ON YOUR FACE, TURNING IT GREEN. **WATCH** OUT FOR YOUR **EYES** AND **MOUTH!**

4. **LOOK** IN THE MIRROR TO SEE YOUR **HULKED-OUT** FACE!

FIN

RAAAARRGH!

17

CRIME TIME!

You have your origin. Now what? *NOW* you figure out *WHY* you fight crime! *TAKE* our quiz, then check the scoring box to discover the *REASON* you fight crime.

1. If you see someone return a library book late, you:

A. remember that oath you took swearing to punish anyone who returned a library book late.

B. keep on moving; you have bigger fish to fry.

2. When your friend crosses the street in the middle instead of at the crosswalk, you:

A. take him to the nearest police station; rules are rules!

B. remind him that it's dangerous and get on with your day.

3. Kang the Conqueror suddenly appears outside your school. You immediately:

A. attack the master of time, then summon the Avengers for backup.

B. stop to ask yourself, "What is Kang doing at my school?"

4. You see someone committing a daring daylight bank robbery. You:

   A. attack the daring daylight bank robber, then summon the Avengers for backup.

   B. nicely ask the robber to put the money back.

5. Your Halloween party is a raging success . . . until the Green Goblin shows up! You:

   A. use your awesome powers to go "bobbing for bad guys" and send Gobby to jail.

   B. figure there's a fifty-fifty chance he's there to take your trick-or-treat candy.

6. Just as you're about to go to sleep, Red Skull smashes through your wall. You:

   A. use your super powers to make short work of your foe.

   B. tell him that he must have the wrong house, and could he please leave through the door?

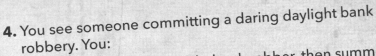

WHAT DID YOU ANSWER?

MOSTLY A'S

If you answered mostly As, you fight crime because you have a very strong sense of right and wrong . . . maybe a little too strong! You believe in justice and that with great power, there must also come great responsibility.

MOSTLY B'S

If you answered mostly Bs, we honestly have no idea why you fight crime—or why you chose mostly Bs, either! But those answers were fun, weren't they? We guess you fight crime because it's what you want to do. You march to the beat of your own drum, and we're good with that!

NOW IT'S TIME TO PUT EVERYTHING TOGETHER! *FILL* IN THE BLANKS IN THE STORY USING THE WORDS IN THE BOX BELOW. *WHEN* YOU'RE DONE, READ YOUR ORIGIN STORY TO A FRIEND . . . OR FOE! (*TRUST* US, THERE'S NOTHING BAD GUYS LIKE *BETTER* THAN LISTENING TO *YOUR* ORIGIN STORY.)

WRITE YOUR OWN ORIGIN?

One day, while walking my dog, I was hit by

__the space phantom__ I was knocked out! Before I knew
(COLUMN A)

it, I woke up to find that I had (a) __time traveling tonge__
(COLUMN B)

What was up with that?

When I walked home, a speeding car almost hit me, but I

__oozed into the__ ! I couldn't believe it.
(COLUMN C) ground

Then I heard __a radioactive__ say, "You must
(COLUMN A) bumble bee

use your __ten fingers on each__ to help people!" Since
(COLUMN B) head

that day, I've dedicated my life to fighting crime and have

__jumped fifty feet__ ever since.
(COLUMN C) in the air

A	B	C
A RADIOACTIVE BUMBLEBEE	TEN FINGERS ON EACH HAND	JUMPED FIFTY FEET IN THE AIR
THE SPACE PHANTOM	TIME-TRAVELING TONGUE	OOZED INTO THE GROUND
A WAVE OF SLEEPINESS	SUPER-SHARP BEAVER TEETH	CHEWED IT TO RIBBONS

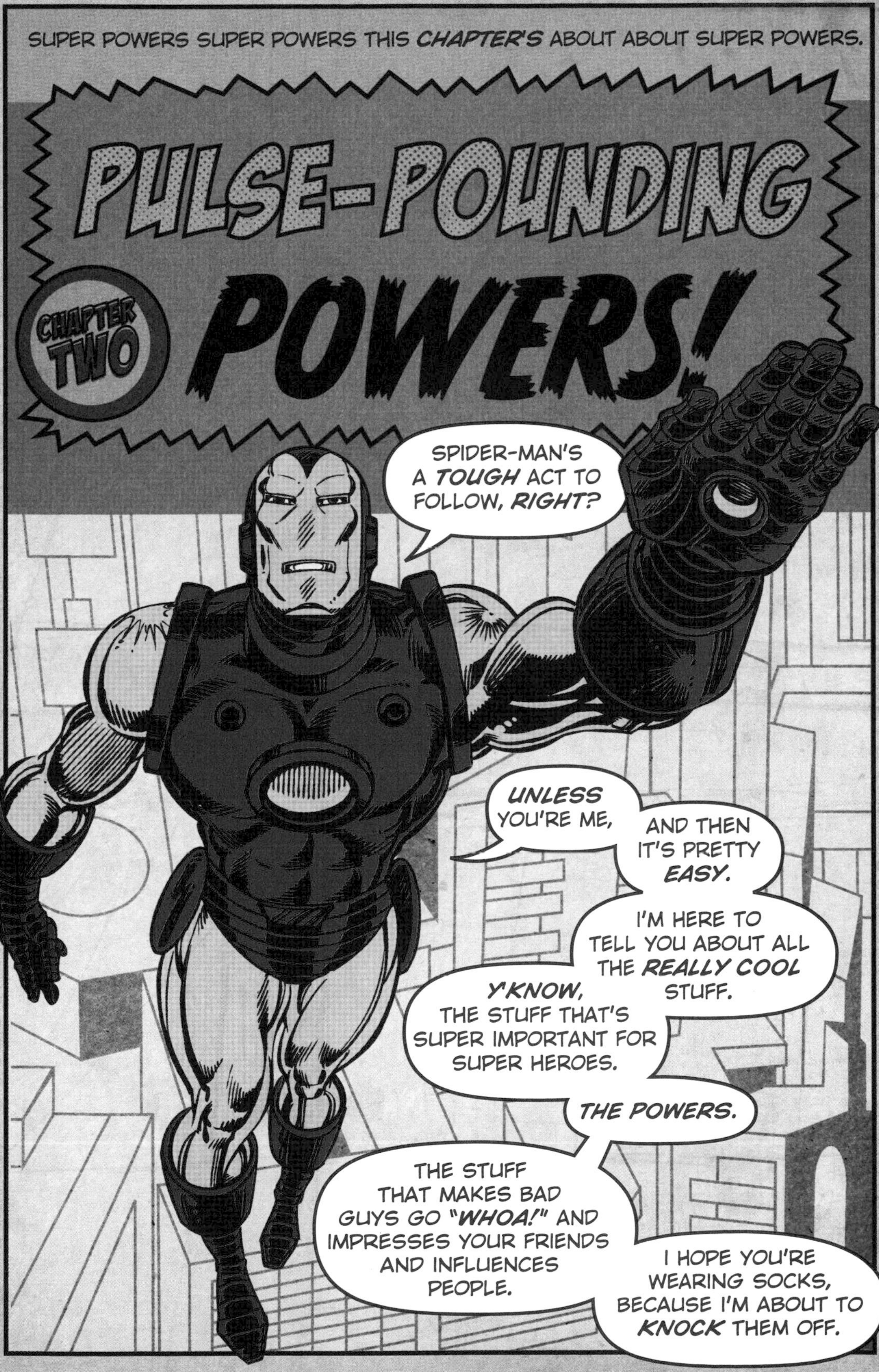
SUPER POWERS SUPER POWERS THIS CHAPTER'S ABOUT ABOUT SUPER POWERS.
PULSE-POUNDING
CHAPTER TWO
POWERS!
SPIDER-MAN'S A TOUGH ACT TO FOLLOW, RIGHT?
UNLESS YOU'RE ME,
AND THEN IT'S PRETTY EASY.
I'M HERE TO TELL YOU ABOUT ALL THE REALLY COOL STUFF.
Y'KNOW, THE STUFF THAT'S SUPER IMPORTANT FOR SUPER HEROES.
THE POWERS.
THE STUFF THAT MAKES BAD GUYS GO "WHOA!" AND IMPRESSES YOUR FRIENDS AND INFLUENCES PEOPLE.
I HOPE YOU'RE WEARING SOCKS, BECAUSE I'M ABOUT TO KNOCK THEM OFF.

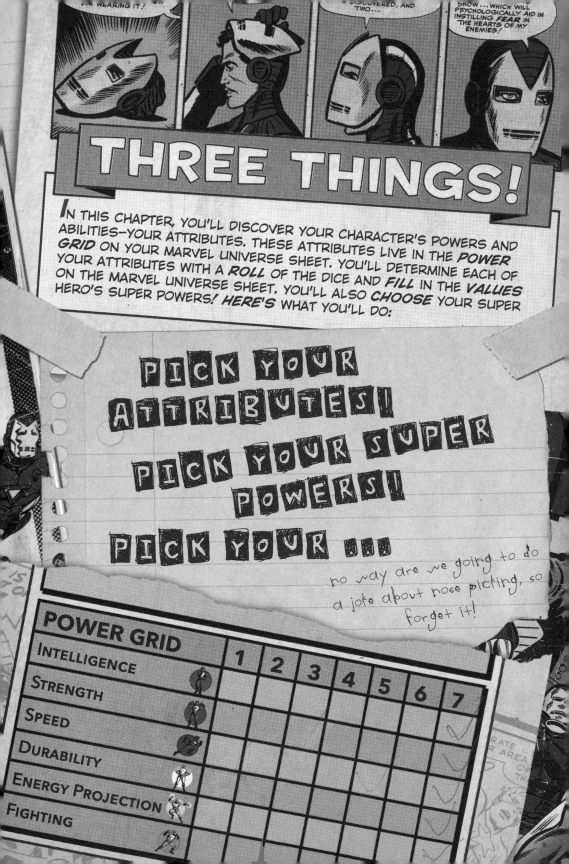

I'M WEARING IT!

...DISCOVERED, AND TWO...

SHOW...WHICH WILL PSYCHOLOGICALLY AID IN INSTILLING *FEAR* IN THE HEARTS OF MY ENEMIES!

THREE THINGS!

IN THIS CHAPTER, YOU'LL DISCOVER YOUR CHARACTER'S POWERS AND ABILITIES—YOUR ATTRIBUTES. THESE ATTRIBUTES LIVE IN THE *POWER GRID* ON YOUR MARVEL UNIVERSE SHEET. YOU'LL DETERMINE EACH OF YOUR ATTRIBUTES WITH A *ROLL* OF THE DICE AND *FILL* IN THE *VALUES* ON THE MARVEL UNIVERSE SHEET. YOU'LL ALSO *CHOOSE* YOUR SUPER HERO'S SUPER POWERS! *HERE'S* WHAT YOU'LL DO:

PICK YOUR ATTRIBUTES!

PICK YOUR SUPER POWERS!

PICK YOUR ...

no way are we going to do a joke about nose picking, so forget it!

POWER GRID		1	2	3	4	5	6	7
INTELLIGENCE								
STRENGTH								
SPEED								
DURABILITY								
ENERGY PROJECTION								
FIGHTING								

INTELLIGENCE

THE **FIRST** THING YOU'LL ENTER INTO YOUR POWER GRID IS YOUR INTELLIGENCE— YOUR **SMARTS!** YOUR ABILITY TO **FIGURE** THINGS OUT, **MAKE** STUFF, COME UP WITH **COOL** GADGETS—THAT'S ALL DETERMINED BY YOUR INTELLIGENCE. THERE ARE **A LOT** OF SMART SUPER HEROES OUT THERE.

ROLL IT!

1. To determine your intelligence, **roll** the number dice.

2. **Roll** the attribute dice. If you land on the intelligence icon, you can **add 1** to your total intelligence score!

3. Turn to **page 165** and fill in the intelligence score in your power grid.

JUST LOOK FOR THE ICON!

It's an *AGE-OLD* debate: who's *STRONGER* than whom? We all want to know if *HULK* can beat *THOR*. But can he beat the *STINK* of a week-old *SALAMI* sandwich? Who *WREAKS* havoc, and who just plain *REEKS*?

STRONGEST HEROES OR ODORS?

10. Captain America

9. Week-old salami sandwich

8. Spider-Man

7. Groot

6. Wet dog

5. Tie: Iron Man/ War Machine

4. She-Hulk

3. That thing in the corner that no one wants to go near

2. Thor

1. Tie: Hulk/ year-old salami sandwich

HEY!

HULK SMELL PRETTY LIKE *ROSES!*

STRENGTH

WHETHER YOUR HERO GETS STRENGTH FROM *MUSCLES* OR A *HIGH-TECH* SUIT OF ARMOR CREATED BY THE *SMARTEST* PERSON *EVER,* * YOU'LL NEED *EVERY* BIT OF IT TO FIGHT THE FORCES OF EVIL. FIND OUT JUST HOW STRONG YOUR CHARACTER IS—LIKE, *"LIFT A CAR"* STRONG OR *"MOVE A MOUNTAIN"* STRONG. HOW DO YOU *STACK* UP?

ROLL IT!

1. To determine your strength, **roll** the number dice.

2. **Roll** the attribute dice. If you land on the strength icon, you can **add 1** to your total strength score!

3. Turn to **page 165** and fill in the strength score in your power grid.

JUST LOOK FOR THE ICON!

25

*ME. TONY STARK. JUST MAKING SURE WE'RE ON THE SAME PAGE.

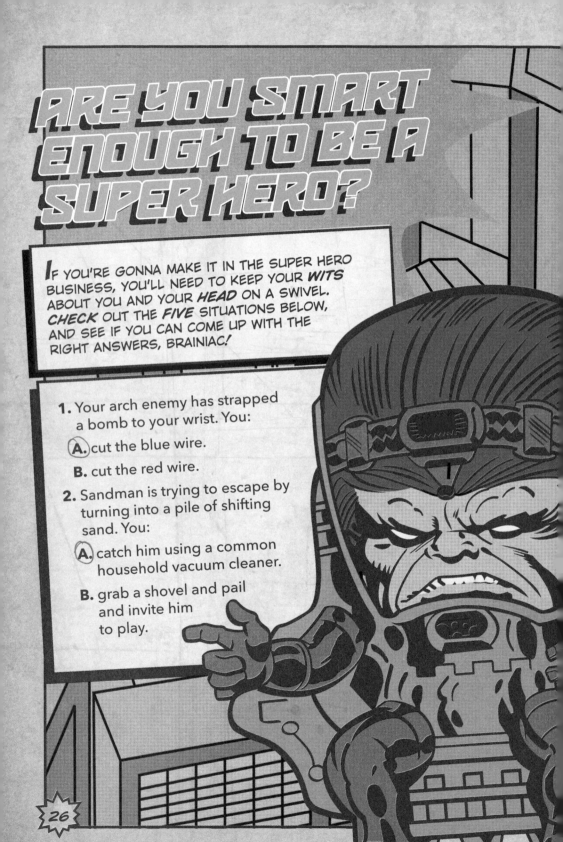

ARE YOU SMART ENOUGH TO BE A SUPER HERO?

IF YOU'RE GONNA MAKE IT IN THE SUPER HERO BUSINESS, YOU'LL NEED TO KEEP YOUR *WITS* ABOUT YOU AND YOUR *HEAD* ON A SWIVEL. *CHECK* OUT THE *FIVE* SITUATIONS BELOW, AND SEE IF YOU CAN COME UP WITH THE RIGHT ANSWERS, BRAINIAC*!*

1. Your arch enemy has strapped a bomb to your wrist. You:

   A. cut the blue wire.

   B. cut the red wire.

2. Sandman is trying to escape by turning into a pile of shifting sand. You:

   A. catch him using a common household vacuum cleaner.

   B. grab a shovel and pail and invite him to play.

3. The police have put out an all-points bulletin on a "snake-themed Super Villain." You:

A. do a quick computer search for known snake-themed Super Villains at large.

B. call the police and tell them that snakes are yucky and there is **NOT A CHANCE** you will help.

4. You just found out that M.O.D.O.K. and the agents of A.I.M. are attacking a nearby laboratory. But you're in the middle of an important history test at school! You:

A. remember that S.H.I.E.L.D. gave you a Life Model Decoy—an exact duplicate of yourself—and you can send it to take the test in your place.

B. remember that your little sister took the Life Model Decoy S.H.I.E.L.D. gave you and dressed it up as one of her Fantastically Gorgeous Horsies.

5. You're facing off against Taskmaster, who can instantly mimic any of your fighting moves. You:

A. dress up like a different Super Hero so he thinks he's fighting someone else and you can trick him by using your own combat moves.

B. dress up like a giant man-eating cow and absolutely terrify Taskmaster, because **WHO ISN'T AFRAID OF A MAN-EATING COW.**

WHAT DID YOU ANSWER?

MOSTLY A'S
If you answered mostly As, you're pretty smart. Not saying the Avengers are gonna give you a call today, but chances are pretty good!

MOSTLY B'S
If you answered mostly Bs, you're . . . *How is it possible that you answered mostly Bs? That can't be right. Is this book broken?!?*

Some people with super speed become *HEROES*. Some . . . *DON'T*. By the numbers, here are the super speedsters who become . . .

SPEED DEMONS!

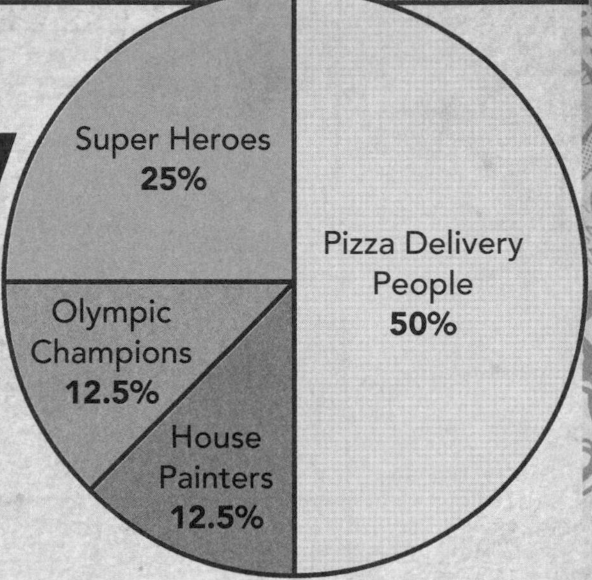

Estimated Numbers by Profession

☐	64,765,875
☐	64
☐	6,432
☐	6,400,032

Super Heroes
25%

Pizza Delivery People
50%

Olympic Champions
12.5%

House Painters
12.5%

SPEED

BIRDS GOTTA FLY, FISH GOTTA SWIM, AND . . . YEAH, I'M NOT SURE WHERE THIS WAS GOING. SO. *SPEED!* IT'S IMPORTANT FOR ALL THE REASONS YOU THINK IT IS. IT'S THE MEASURE OF HOW FAST YOUR SUPER HERO CAN DO SOMETHING, HOW QUICKLY YOU CAN MOVE. THEN GET READY TO ROLL.

ROLL IT!

1. To determine your speed, **roll** the number dice.

2. **Roll** the attribute dice. If you land on the speed icon, you can **add 1** to your total speed score!

3. Turn to **page 165** and fill in the speed score in your power grid.

JUST LOOK FOR THE ICON!

*Y*OUR MISSION: *DESIGN* A SUIT OF ARMOR, USING PACKING BUBBLES AND A CARDBOARD BOX, THAT CAN PREVENT AN EGG FROM *BREAKING!* THIS ACTIVITY CAN BE A *LITTLE* MESSY. *ASK* A PARENT OR GUARDIAN FOR HELP, AND *TRY* DOING THIS ONE OVER A BATHTUB!

WHAT YOU'LL NEED

- Packing bubbles (the kind used to send packages)
- A small cardboard box (like a shoebox)
- Tape
- One dozen (that's twelve, count 'em, twelve) eggs

THE SETUP

1. TAKE *ONE* EGG OUT OF THE CARTON.

2. GENTLY *WRAP* THE EGG IN PACKING BUBBLES, THEN *PLACE* INSIDE THE CARDBOARD BOX. *MAKE* SURE THE EGG DOESN'T MOVE. *TAPE* THE BOX CLOSED.

3. *DROP* THE BOX FROM A HEIGHT OF ABOUT *FOUR* FEET OVER THE TUB. *OPEN* THE BOX, AND SEE *IF* YOUR EGG *SURVIVED!*

4. *IF* YOU BREAK AN EGG, KEEP TRYING DIFFERENT WAYS OF PACKING THE NEXT EGG *UNTIL* YOU FIND THE PERFECT SUIT OF EGG ARMOR.

FIN

DURABILITY

DURABILITY. IT'S A WORD THAT MEANS *SOMETHING* IF YOU LOOK IT UP IN A DICTIONARY. FOR OUR PURPOSES, IT MEANS HOW *TOUGH* YOUR HERO IS. *HOW* MUCH DAMAGE YOU CAN TAKE. *HOW* MUCH *"GET UP* AND *GO"* YOU HAVE.

ROLL IT!

1. To determine your durability, **roll** the number dice.

2. **Roll** the attribute dice. If you land on the durability icon, you can **add 1** to your total durability score!

3. Turn to **page 165** and fill in the durability score in your power grid.

JUST LOOK FOR THE ICON!

THIS CHAPTER IS *FULL* OF IMPORTANT ACTIVITIES. YOU'RE CHOOSING *ALL* YOUR ATTRIBUTES, FOR *CRYING* OUT LOUD! BUT THERE'S SOMETHING ELSE YOU NEED TO DO. YOU NEED TO *CHOOSE* YOUR POWERS! CAN YOU *FLY?* DO YOU *STICK* TO WALLS LIKE A CERTAIN ANNOYING ARACHNID? DO YOU *WEAR* A NIGH-INDESTRUCTIBLE SUIT OF POWERED ARMOR LIKE TONY STARK, WHOM WE HAVE ESTABLISHED TO BE THE *SMARTEST* PERSON EVER?

PICK YOUR POWER!

WHAT YOU NEED TO DO:
TO PICK YOUR POWER SET, YOU'LL NEED BOTH DICE. GIVE THEM A ROLL TOGETHER. NOW TAKE A LOOK AT THE CHART ON *PAGE 33*. PICK ONE POWER BENEATH EACH OF THE TWO ROLLS YOU MADE. WRITE THEM IN THE SPACE PROVIDED ON THE MARVEL UNIVERSE SHEET ON PAGE *165!*

YOU CAN ALSO WRITE IN YOUR *OWN* POWERS USING THE *BLANK* SPACES!

① ATTRIBUTES!

1. INTELLIGENCE

SUPER SMARTS
COMPUTER BRAIN

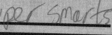

super smarts

2. STRENGTH

GAMMA MUSCLES
AUGMENTED INSECT
STRENGTH

augmented insect strength

3. SPEED

FLIGHT
SUPER-FAST
RUNNING

super fast running

4. DURABILITY

POWERED ARMOR
ENDLESS ENERGY

5. ENERGY PROJECTION

POWER BLASTS
PSYCHIC BOLTS

6. FIGHTING

SUPER-SOLDIER SKILLS
MARTIAL-ARTS
MASTERY

② SPECIAL POWERS!

ENHANCED HEARING
OWL VISION

EATING CAKE, SO
MUCH CAKE
TOUCHING
PORCUPINES AND
NOT GET HURT

SIPHONING ENERGY
FROM VILLAINS
BATTING EYELASHES
AT SUPER SPEED

CONJURING
DEMONS, CUTE CATS
RADIOACTIVE
ELBOWS

TURNING BREAKFAST
INTO DINNER
TURNING DINNER
INTO BREAKFAST

SWIMMING AS FAST
AS 3.5 SHARKS
UNDERWATER
BREATHING

e.   he's a menace, pla...   Man's a wall-crawling menace
a   A wall-crawling menace! And a   and a weasel.
  weasel. Blah, blah, blah, Spider-

DEAR TONY
Hot Stuff!

BY GENIUS INVENTOR AND ALL-AROUND LOVABLE BILLIONAIRE TONY STARK

DEAR TONY, I love science so much. Just like you, all I want is to make the world a better place, and by "better place," I mean a place that's better for me. My question is, I am working on a very big, let's call it a "device" that harnesses the heat of the earth's core. How much energy is required to melt Iron Man's armor, not that I'd do that?

SIGNED, SO NOT A VILLAIN

DEAR SO, Any device that can harness the heat of the earth's core could project tremendous energy and benefit humanity. In order to answer your question, we would need to send all of the Avengers—even Ant-Man—to your home to assess the situation. We'll be there in five!

SIGNED, TONY

Everyone has a problem. What is yours? For a personal reply, write to genius inventor and all-around lovable billionaire Tony Stark, Box 55555, Glendale, CA 91201 and enclose a stamped, self-addressed envelope.

Happy Little Trees

THERE'S A LOT OF HAPPINESS TO BE HAD WHEN YOU PAINT. IT'S ALMOST LIKE IT'S A JOY OR SOMETHING.

BY ROSS ROBERTS

Well, shoot, let's just make a little creek right here. Now maybe take a little of our alizarin crimson and go into our phthalo blue. That's gonna make a really pretty color. Take your palette knife and just put your creek wherever it wants to live.

all
ly
er
no
rol
ew.
!!

ENERGY PROJECTION

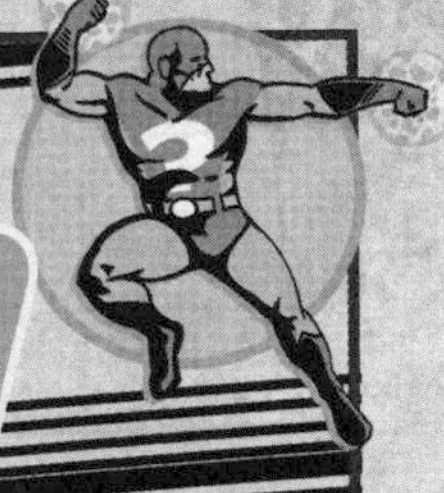

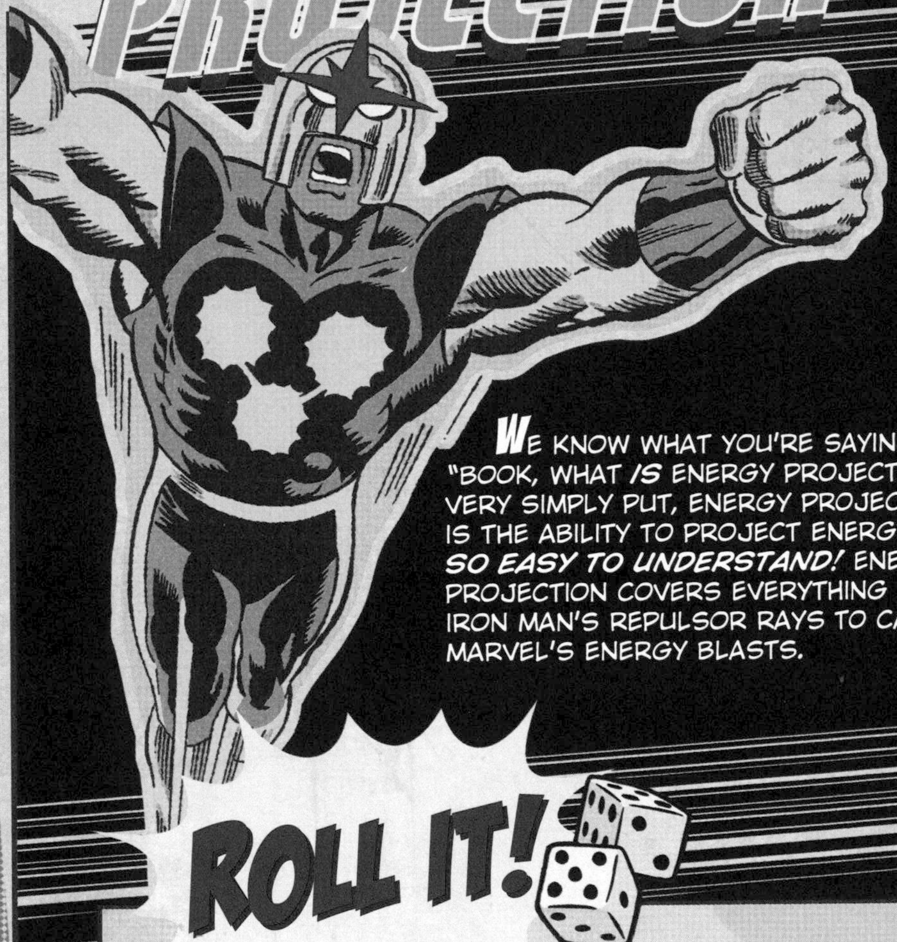

W**E KNOW WHAT YOU'RE SAYING:* "BOOK, WHAT *IS* ENERGY PROJECTION?" VERY SIMPLY PUT, ENERGY PROJECTION IS THE ABILITY TO PROJECT ENERGY. ***IT IS SO EASY TO UNDERSTAND! ENERGY PROJECTION COVERS EVERYTHING FROM IRON MAN'S REPULSOR RAYS TO CAPTAIN MARVEL'S ENERGY BLASTS.

ROLL IT!

1. To determine your energy projection, **roll** the number dice.
2. **Roll** the attribute dice. If you land on the energy projection icon, you can **add 1** to your total energy projection score!
3. Turn to **page 165** and fill in the energy projection score in your power grid.

JUST LOOK FOR THE 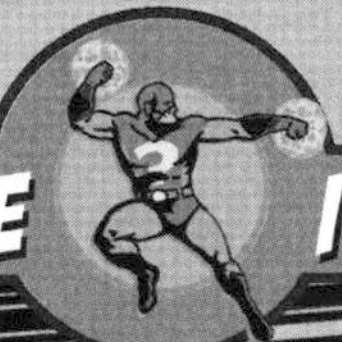 **ICON!**

MAKE YOUR OWN

FLASHLIGHT REPULSOR RAYS!

- Two small flashlights—the smaller the better!
- A pair of gloves or mittens
- A roll of duct tape (**WARNING:** Please note we said **duct** tape, not **duck** tape. We are not taping ducks here.)

THE SETUP

PLACE *ONE* FLASHLIGHT ON THE *BACK* OF EACH GLOVE.

PUT A HAND INSIDE *ONE* GLOVE, AND USE A PIECE OF DUCT TAPE TO *SECURE* THE FLASHLIGHT IN PLACE.

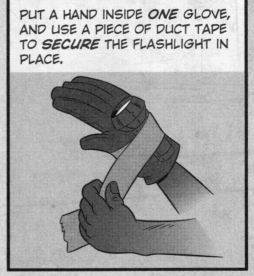

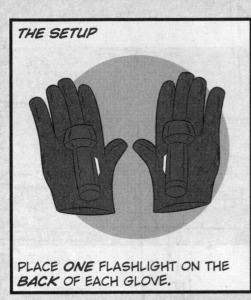

REPEAT THIS STEP WITH THE OTHER GLOVE.

TURN OUT THE *LIGHTS*, AND TURN ON THE *FLASHLIGHTS*. YOU'RE READY TO *ZAP* YOUR REPULSOR RAYS ALL OVER THE PLACE!

FIN

SOME HEROES HAVE *POWERS*, AND OTHERS RELY ON *GADGETS* AND *WEAPONS* TO AID THEM IN THEIR BATTLE AGAINST THE BAD GUYS. LET'S SEE IF YOU CAN *MATCH* THE SUPER HEROES TO THEIR GADGETS OR WEAPONS. *BONUS* POINTS IF YOU CAN MATCH SPIDER-MAN WITH HIS *FAVORITE* BREAKFAST FOOD.*

WEAPON OF CHOICE

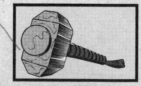
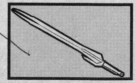

*WE REALIZE THIS HAS NOTHING TO DO WITH WEAPONS. WE *REALLY* DO. BUT WE *LOVE* BREAKFAST.

FIGHTING

WELL, *THAT'S* PUTTING IT BLUNTLY! *FIGHTING* IS EXACTLY WHAT YOU THINK IT IS. *IT'S* A MEASURE OF YOUR HERO'S ABILITY TO *MIX* IT UP WITH THE VILLAINS, TO *BLOCK* BLOWS AND *LAND* A PUNCH THAT WILL SAVE THE DAY. *NOT* ALL HEROES EXCEL AT FIGHTING. *WILL* YOU MAKE THE GRADE?

ROLL IT!

1. To determine your fighting, **roll** the number dice.

2. **Roll** the attribute dice. If you land on the fighting icon, you can **add 1** to your total fighting score!

3. Turn to **page 165** and fill in the fighting score in your power grid.

JUST LOOK FOR THE ICON!

39

WHAT HAVE WE LEARNED SO FAR—OTHER THAN THE FACT THAT *SPIDER-MAN* REALLY. LIKES WHEAT CAKES FOR BREAKFAST? *TEST* YOURSELF WITH THIS QUICK QUIZ, AND THEN MOVE ON TO *CHAPTER THREE!*

POWER PLAY!

1 Who's the more skilled fighter?

OR

2 What kind of tape did you use for the activity on page 37?

DUCT TAPE **OR** **SCOTCH TAPE**

3 Which of the following is **NOT** one of your hero's attributes?

SPEED **OR** **SLEEPINESS**

4 What percentage of people who acquire super speed deliver pizza?

50% **OR** **15%**

5 Two trains leave New York City at the same time. One train is traveling thirty miles per hour, the other fifty miles per hour. What train will arrive on the moon first?

ANSWERS:
1) Black Widow, 2) Duct tape, 3) Sleepiness, 4) 50%, 5) Don't worry, we fired the person who wrote that question. If you answered even none of the questions correctly, congratulations! This isn't school!

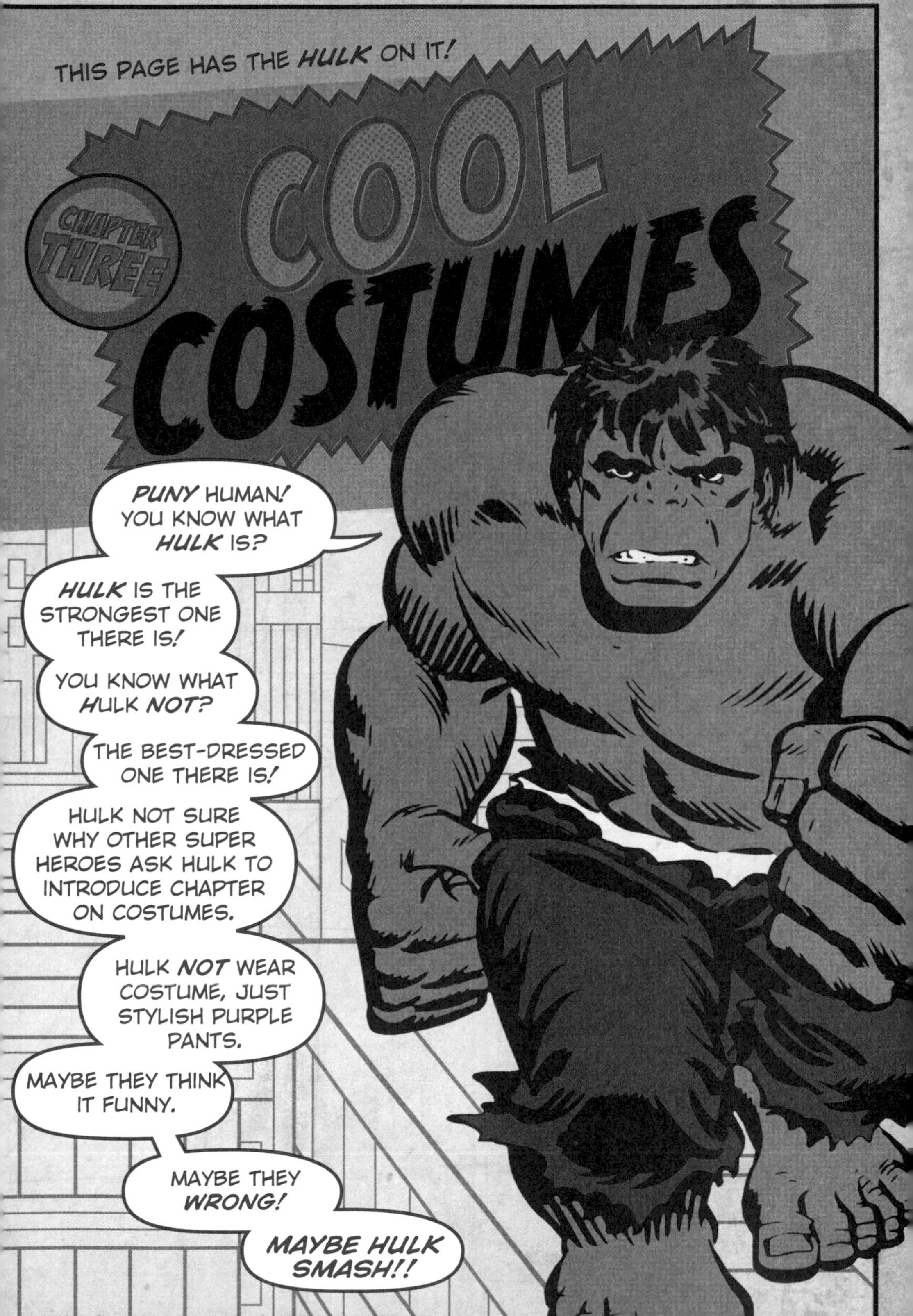
THIS PAGE HAS THE HULK ON IT!
CHAPTER THREE
COOL COSTUMES
PUNY HUMAN! YOU KNOW WHAT HULK IS?
HULK IS THE STRONGEST ONE THERE IS!
YOU KNOW WHAT HULK NOT?
THE BEST-DRESSED ONE THERE IS!
HULK NOT SURE WHY OTHER SUPER HEROES ASK HULK TO INTRODUCE CHAPTER ON COSTUMES.
HULK NOT WEAR COSTUME, JUST STYLISH PURPLE PANTS.
MAYBE THEY THINK IT FUNNY.
MAYBE THEY WRONG!
MAYBE HULK SMASH!!
ANYWAY, FIND OUT ALL ABOUT MAKING SUPER HERO COSTUMES AND OTHER STUFF.

TWO THINGS!

*T*HE CLOTHES MAKE THE HERO! WHETHER IT'S A SUIT OF HIGH-TECH ARMOR OR A PAIR OF TORN PURPLE PANTS, IT'S UP TO YOU TO DECIDE WHAT YOUR HERO WILL WEAR WHEN YOU SAVE THE DAY. *DISCOVER* THE FASCINATING HISTORY OF THE SUPER HERO COSTUME, AND *GET READY* TO CREATE YOUR VERY OWN SUPER HERO COSTUME TO ADD TO YOUR MARVEL UNIVERSE SHEET. *FACE FRONT*, TRUE BELIEVER. IN THIS CHAPTER:

DESIGN YOUR VERY OWN SUPER HERO COSTUME!

Wait, we already said that, yes? Okay.
Well, you'll be doing that, then!

Settling on your Super Hero costume
means it's finally time to . . .

choose your super hero name!

THEY CAN'T ALL BE GOLD. FOR EVERY SPECTACULAR NAME LIKE *SPIDER-MAN, HULK,* OR *BLACK WIDOW,* THERE'S A NAME THAT'S . . . LESS SPECTACULAR. *BELOW,* YOU'LL FIND THE TOP *TEN* REJECTED SUPER HERO NAMES. *APOLOGIES* TO ANY HEROES WHO FIND THEIR NAMES ON THE LIST.

REJECTED SUPER HERO NAMES

10. Zooface

9. Pineapple Pete

8. The Cosmic Tummy

7. Simi-Ann, the woman who walks like a monkey

6. The Waiterinator

5. Guppy

4. The Mighty Utensils (Forkboy, the Spoon, Jack the Knife)

3. Doctor Smells

2. Captain Colonel

1. Ant-man

COME ON, WHO PUT MY NAME ON THE LIST?

SPIDER-MAN?

LOOK, JUST BECAUSE I DIDN'T HELP INTRODUCE *CHAPTER ONE* IS NO REASON TO MAKE FUN OF ME.

SYMBOLS MATCH

WHEN YOU'RE THINKING ABOUT IDEAS FOR YOUR COSTUME, IT *HELPS* TO LOOK AT SOME OF THE *AWESOME* APPAREL WORN BY YOUR *FAVORITE* SUPER HEROES. YOU CAN *FIND* SOME *INSPIRATION* WHILE YOU MATCH THESE *SUPER HEROES* WITH THEIR *ICONS!*

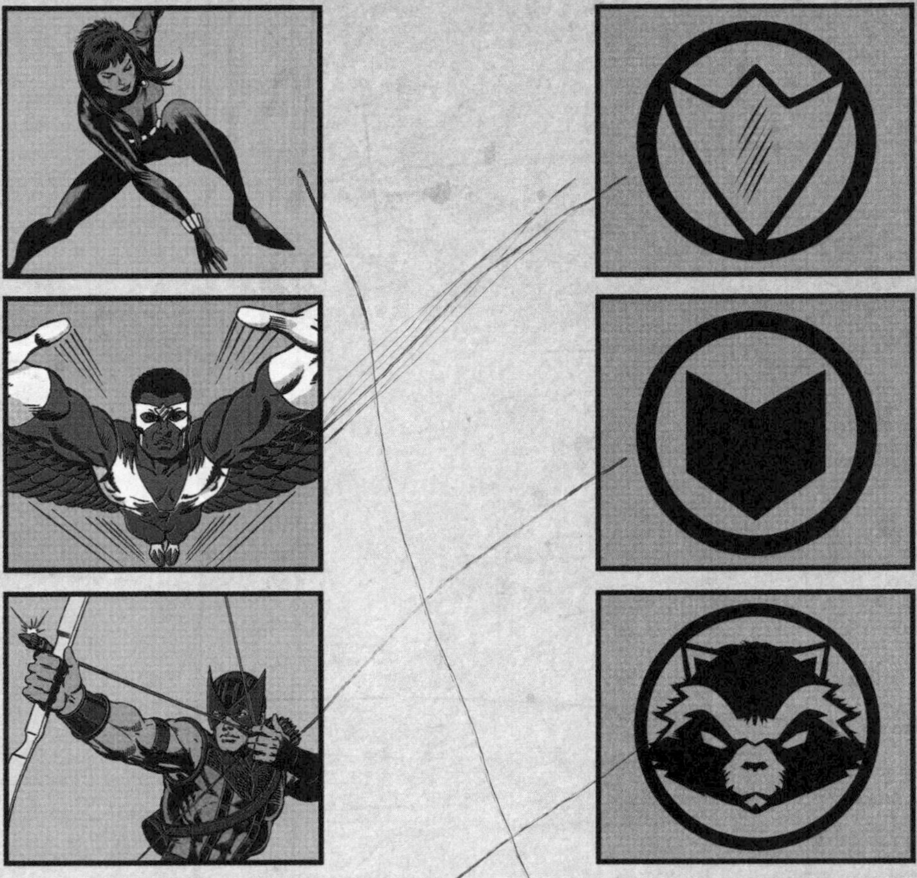

ANSWERS:

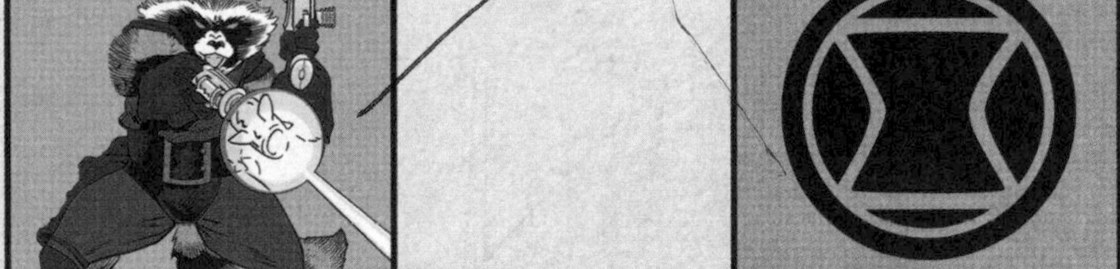

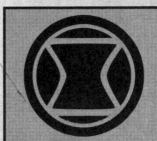

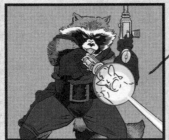

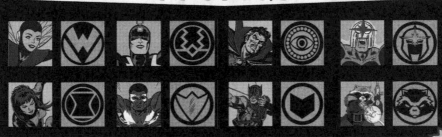

SOME HEROES DON'T MIND EVERYONE KNOWING *WHO* THEY ARE. *BUT* MOST LIKE TO KEEP THEIR IDENTITIES A SECRET. AND THE *BEST* WAY TO KEEP YOUR IDENTITY A SECRET IS TO KEEP YOUR FACE COVERED! JUST FOLLOW THE STEPS BELOW AND YOU'LL HAVE YOUR OWN SUPER HERO MASK IN NO TIME.

MARVELOUS MASKS

WHAT YOU'LL NEED

- A ski mask
- An old black sock (ask your parents for one)
- A white scarf
- Felt in various colors
- Permanent or fabric markers
- Scissors
- Nontoxic fabric glue

THE SETUP

START BY SKETCHING OUT YOUR IDEAS FOR THE THREE DIFFERENT MASK MODELS.

USE THE SCISSORS TO CUT OUT FELT SHAPES, AND THEN USE FABRIC GLUE TO STICK THEM TO YOUR MASK.

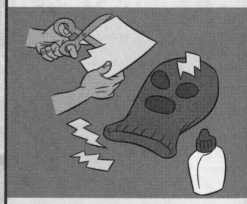

CHECK OUT THE HERO HINTS ON PAGE 47 FOR DIFFERENT MASKS!

HERO HINT #1

SKI MASK

THIS ONE IS PROBABLY THE *EASIEST* TO MAKE, SINCE IT'S PRETTY MUCH DONE ALREADY! ONCE YOU HAVE THE FELT GLUED IN PLACE, YOU'RE READY TO *ROCK!*

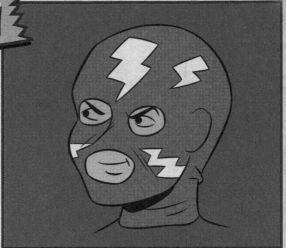

HERO HINT #2

SOCK MASK

ASK A PARENT OR GUARDIAN TO HELP YOU CUT EYEHOLES FOR THIS MASK. THEY CAN ALSO HELP YOU TIE THE MASK IN PLACE.

HERO HINT #3

SCARF MASK

YOU CAN USE THE PERMANENT OR FABRIC MARKERS TO DECORATE AND DESIGN THIS MASK. WHEN YOU'RE DONE, *ASK* A PARENT OR GUARDIAN OR FRIEND OR TALKING TREE MAN TO *TIE* IT IN PLACE.

It can be an *EMBARRASSING* moment for a super hero, showing up for a big super villain showdown only to find *ANOTHER* hero wearing the same costume. *BELOW* you'll meet some heroes who have worn variations on the same costume. It's up to you to judge . . .

WHO WORE IT BETTER?

Tony Stark / **James Rhodes**

Hank Pym / **Scott Lang**

Peter Parker / **Peter Porker**

Chuck and Hal Chandler / **Delroy Garrett**

HOW THEY DID IT

NO ONE SAID THAT COMING UP WITH A COSTUME WOULD BE *EASY*. *HERE'S* A LITTLE BEHIND-THE-SCENES INSIGHT INTO SUPER HERO COSTUMES.

> LET THE RECORD SHOW THAT IRON MAN HAS MORE LOOKS THAN *ANYBODY*.

IRON MAN	*Took inspiration from junk lying around to build impressive wearable tank*
WASP	*Created so many costumes that this entire book could easily be devoted to them*
KA-ZAR	*Grabbed a loincloth, called it a costume*
POWER MAN	*Has come up with several costumes, because he's bulletproof but clothes aren't*
DOCTOR STRANGE	*Traded in surgeon's clothing for mystic cloak given to him by the Ancient One*
SPIDER-MAN	*Despite showing no prior artistic ability whatsoever, designed and sewed own costume*

PETER PARKER PRETTY MUCH KNEW THAT HE WAS GOING TO MAKE A SPIDER-THEMED COSTUME. *NO* MYSTERY THERE. IT'S *NOT* LIKE HE WAS BITTEN BY A *RADIOACTIVE PARASTRATIOSPHECOMYIA STRATIOSPHECOMYIOIDES!** BUT IF YOU'RE TRYING TO FIGURE OUT WHAT KIND OF COSTUME TO MAKE, YOU COULD DO *WORSE* THAN GENERATING ONE COMPLETELY . . .

@RANDOM

HERE'S WHAT YOU DO:

1. GET YOUR NUMBER DICE. *ADMIRE* THE CRAFTSMANSHIP.

2. FOR EACH COLUMN (*MASK, TORSO, ARMS*, ETC.), YOU'LL ROLL THE DICE. *LOOK* FOR THE ITEM NEXT TO THE NUMBER YOU ROLLED.

3. WASH, RINSE, REPEAT. *WAIT*, YOU'RE NOT WASHING YOUR HAIR. *JUST* REPEAT STEP *2* THEN, UNTIL YOU'RE DONE!

I LIKE MY COSTUMES *FUNKY!*

**HA!* BUG SCIENTISTS LOVE THIS JOKE!

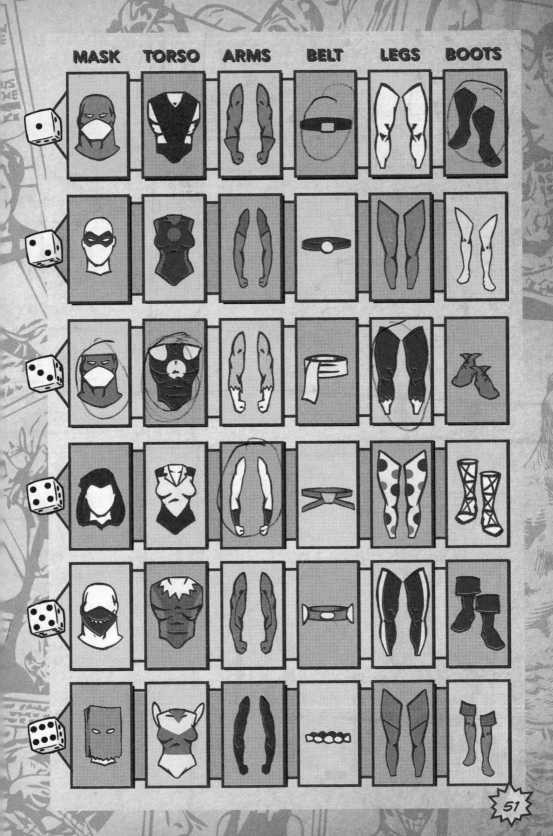

MASK TORSO ARMS BELT LEGS BOOTS

51

WE'VE GIVEN YOU LOTS OF IDEAS FOR YOUR SUPER HERO COSTUME, AND NOW IT'S TIME TO COMMIT! TURN TO THE MARVEL UNIVERSE PROFILE ON PAGE 167. YOU'LL FIND A BLANK PAGE. USE THAT TO DRAW IN YOUR SUPER HERO'S COSTUME. YOU CAN USE THE IDEAS FROM PAGE 51 OR FROM ANY OF THE OTHER ACTIVITIES IN THIS CHAPTER.

FINAL FASHIONS

BUT WAIT! THERE'S MORE! (WE'VE ALWAYS WANTED TO SAY THAT.) GRAB YOUR ATTRIBUTE DICE. GIVE IT A ROLL, AND CHECK THE TABLE BELOW. THIS IS YOUR COSTUME'S SPECIAL FEATURE. YOU'LL WANT TO WRITE THIS DOWN IN THE SPACE BENEATH YOUR COSTUME DRAWING ON PAGE 167.

1	MINIATURE PORTAL THAT FOLDS TIME AND SPACE
2	EMERGENCY POWER SOURCE
3	CAPSULE THAT RELEASES PYM PARTICLES, ENABLING WEARER TO SHRINK
4	IMPERVIOUSNESS TO ALL SMALL-ARMS FIRE
5	SATELLITE COMMUNICATIONS SYSTEM
6	EXTRA SOCKS

FUNNY, I DON'T SEE MY COSTUME ANYWHERE IN THIS BOOK.

DID YOU KNOW *MANY* SUPER HEROES HAVE NAMES INSPIRED BY ANIMALS? *VERY* FEW SUPER HEROES HAVE NAMES INSPIRED BY MAJOR APPLIANCES. YOU ARE MORE LIKELY TO MEET A *SPIDER-MAN* OR A *BLACK PANTHER* THAN YOU ARE A *RAGING REFRIGERATOR* OR A *BLUE BLENDER*. CHECK OUT THE NAMES OF ALL THESE ANIMAL-THEMED GOOD GUYS.

ANIMAL INSTINCT

FALCON

WASP

SPIDER-WOMAN

BLACK WIDOW

SQUIRREL GIRL

ROCKET RACCOON

ANT-MAN

BLACK PANTHER

SPIDER-MAN

A SUPER HERO NEEDS A ***SHARP*** MIND, READY TO POUNCE ON ANY THREAT. KEEP YOUR MIND ***MARVELOUS*** BY FINDING THE NAMES OF THESE ***TEN*** SUPER HEROES HIDDEN IN THE GRID TO THE RIGHT. BONUS POINTS IF YOU CAN ALSO FIND THE ***ONE*** SECRET IDENTITY WE SNUCK INTO THE GRID!

HELLO, MY NAME IS . . .

MS. MARVEL

CAPTAIN MARVEL

SPIDER-MAN

HULK

SQUIRREL GIRL

DR. STRANGE

FALCON

HAWKEYE

WASP

THOR

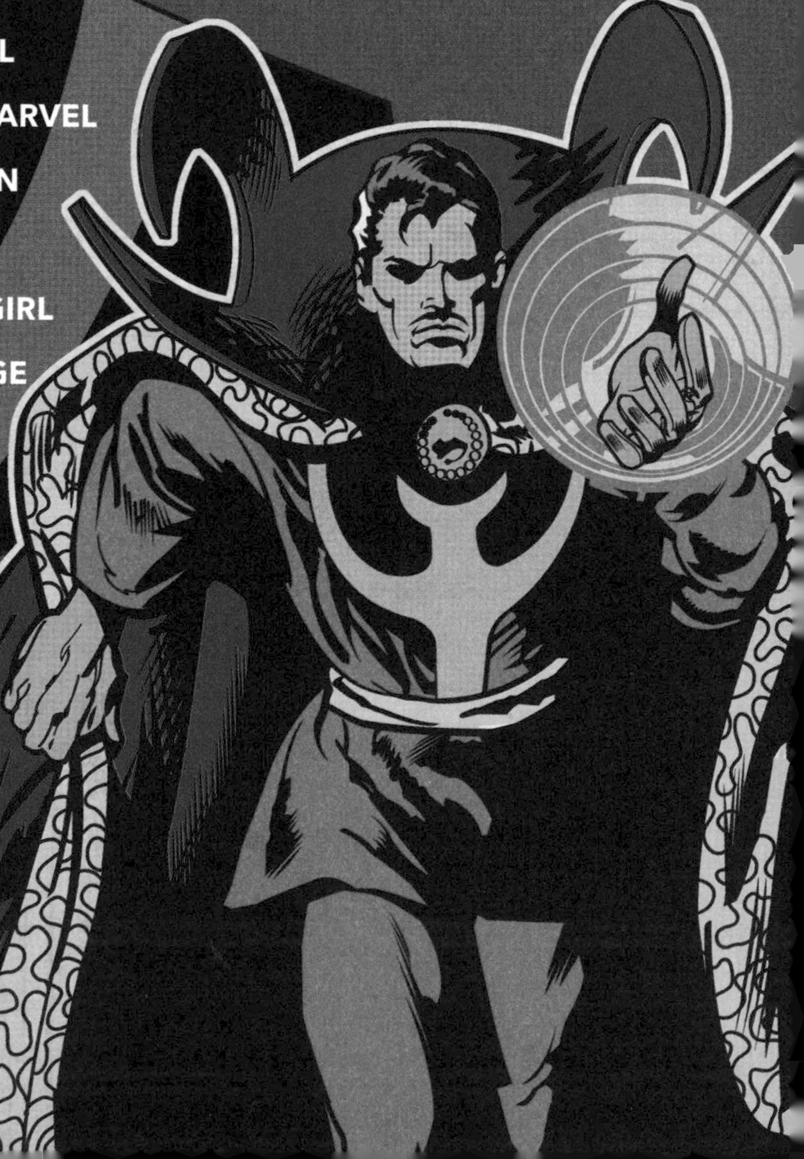

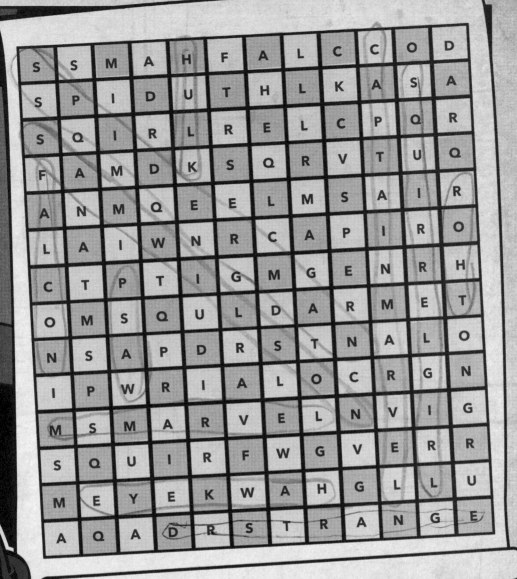

S	S	M	A	H	F	A	L	C	C	O	D
S	P	I	D	U	T	H	L	K	A	S	A
S	Q	I	R	L	R	E	L	C	P	Q	R
F	A	M	D	K	S	Q	R	V	T	U	Q
A	N	M	Q	E	E	L	M	S	A	I	R
L	A	I	W	N	R	C	A	P	I	R	O
C	T	P	T	I	G	M	G	E	N	R	H
O	M	S	Q	U	L	D	A	R	M	E	T
N	S	A	P	D	R	S	T	N	A	L	O
I	P	W	R	I	A	L	O	C	R	G	N
M	S	M	A	R	V	E	L	N	V	I	G
S	Q	U	I	R	F	W	G	V	E	R	R
M	E	Y	E	K	W	A	H	G	L	L	U
A	Q	A	D	R	S	T	R	A	N	G	E

HERO HINT!

LOOK FOR WORDS FORWARD AND *BACKWARD*, UP AND DOWN, AND DIAGONALLY.

ANSWERS:

IT'S TIME TO—YOU *GUESSED* IT—CHOOSE YOUR SUPER HERO NAME. YOU MAY ALREADY HAVE AN *AWESOME* IDEA FOR YOUR NAME, SOMETHING THAT WILL STRIKE *FEAR* INTO THE HEARTS OF *EVILDOERS*. IF THAT'S THE CASE, TURN TO PAGE *165* RIGHT NOW AND FILL IN YOUR HERO NAME ON YOUR MARVEL UNIVERSE SHEET! *BUT* IF YOU COULD STILL USE A LITTLE HELP, WE HAVE JUST THE THING.

NAME THAT NAME!

WHAT YOU NEED TO DO: GET YOUR ATTRIBUTE AND NUMBER DICE. BE *NICE* TO THEM. THEY'VE HAD A LONG DAY. *ROLL* THEM BOTH. *FIND* THE SYMBOL AND NUMBER ON THE NEXT PAGE. THEN *PICK* ONE WORD BENEATH EACH. THAT, MY FRIEND, IS YOUR SUPER HERO NAME! *WRITE* IT IN THE SPACE ON YOUR MARVEL UNIVERSE SHEET.

YOU CAN ALSO WRITE IN YOUR *OWN* NAMES USING THE *BLANK* SPACES!

① ATTRIBUTES!

1. INTELLIGENCE

BLUE
BLACK
PUCE

2. STRENGTH

DARK
GRIM
SENSIBLE

3. SPEED

CAPTAIN
COMMANDER
PRIVATE

4. DURABILITY

DOCTOR
PROFESSOR
INTERN

5. ENERGY PROJECTION

RED
GREEN
OFF-WHITE

6. FIGHTING

LIGHTNING
THUNDER
RAIN

② SPECIAL POWERS!

FREEDOM
PROTECTOR
VACUUMER

KARATE
KICK
THUMB

Karate

WOMAN
LASS
LADY

MAN
BOY
KID

DEFENDER
ANNIHILATOR
MILLIONAIRE

Defender

MISTER
MISS
PRESIDENT

57

THE WORST SUPER HERO COSTUMES!

YOU'VE HEARD OF BAD HAIR DAYS, RIGHT? *WELL*, SOMETIMES SUPER HEROES HAVE *BAD* COSTUME DAYS. *MAYBE* THEIR SUIT WAS DIRTY, *MAYBE* IT WAS AT THE CLEANERS, MAYBE *RED SKULL* DESTROYED IT OR *SOLD* IT TO THE *MASTERS OF EVIL*. YOU *NEVER* KNOW. BUT WHAT WE DO KNOW IS THAT THESE COSTUMES WERE ABSOLUTELY *THE WORST*.

ONCE UPON A TIME, THE *SUPER-SOLDIER SERUM* IN *CAPTAIN AMERICA'S* SYSTEM STARTED BREAKING DOWN. *TO* AUGMENT HIS STRENGTH, *TONY STARK* GAVE *CAP* THIS VERY UNCOMFORTABLE-LOOKING SUIT OF ARMOR.

WHEN SPIDER-MAN WAS INVITED TO APPEAR ON A POPULAR LATE-NIGHT TALK SHOW, HE REALIZED HOW *DIRTY* HIS COSTUME WAS. SO PETER HAD TO *IMPROVISE* A COSTUME WHILE HE *WASHED* HIS ONLY SPIDEY SUIT!

THOR. THOR, THOR, THOR. *WHAT HAPPENED?*

59

BEFORE YOU CAN MOVE ON TO THE NEXT PHASE OF CREATING YOUR SUPER HERO, YOU **NEED** TO TAKE THIS QUICK QUIZ TO MAKE SURE YOU'VE LEARNED ALL YOU **NEED** TO KNOW.

CASE CLOTHES-D!

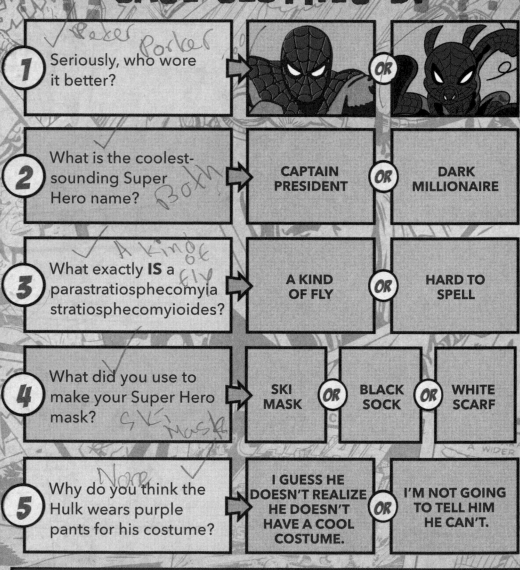

1 Seriously, who wore it better?   ~Peter Porter~   OR

2 What is the coolest-sounding Super Hero name?   ~Both~   CAPTAIN PRESIDENT   OR   DARK MILLIONAIRE

3 What exactly **IS** a parastratiosphecomyia stratiosphecomyioides?   ~A Kind of fly~   A KIND OF FLY   OR   HARD TO SPELL

4 What did you use to make your Super Hero mask?   ~Ski Mask~   SKI MASK   OR   BLACK SOCK   OR   WHITE SCARF

5 Why do you think the Hulk wears purple pants for his costume?   ~None~   I GUESS HE DOESN'T REALIZE HE DOESN'T HAVE A COOL COSTUME.   OR   I'M NOT GOING TO TELL HIM HE CAN'T.

ANSWERS:
1) Spider-Ham, 2) Tie between Captain President/Dark Millionaire, 3) It's a kind of fly, 4) If you did the activity, we'll assume it's one of these three, 5) Because that's how the artists draw him, silly. If you answered any of these questions differently—and really, how couldn't you?—it's all good!

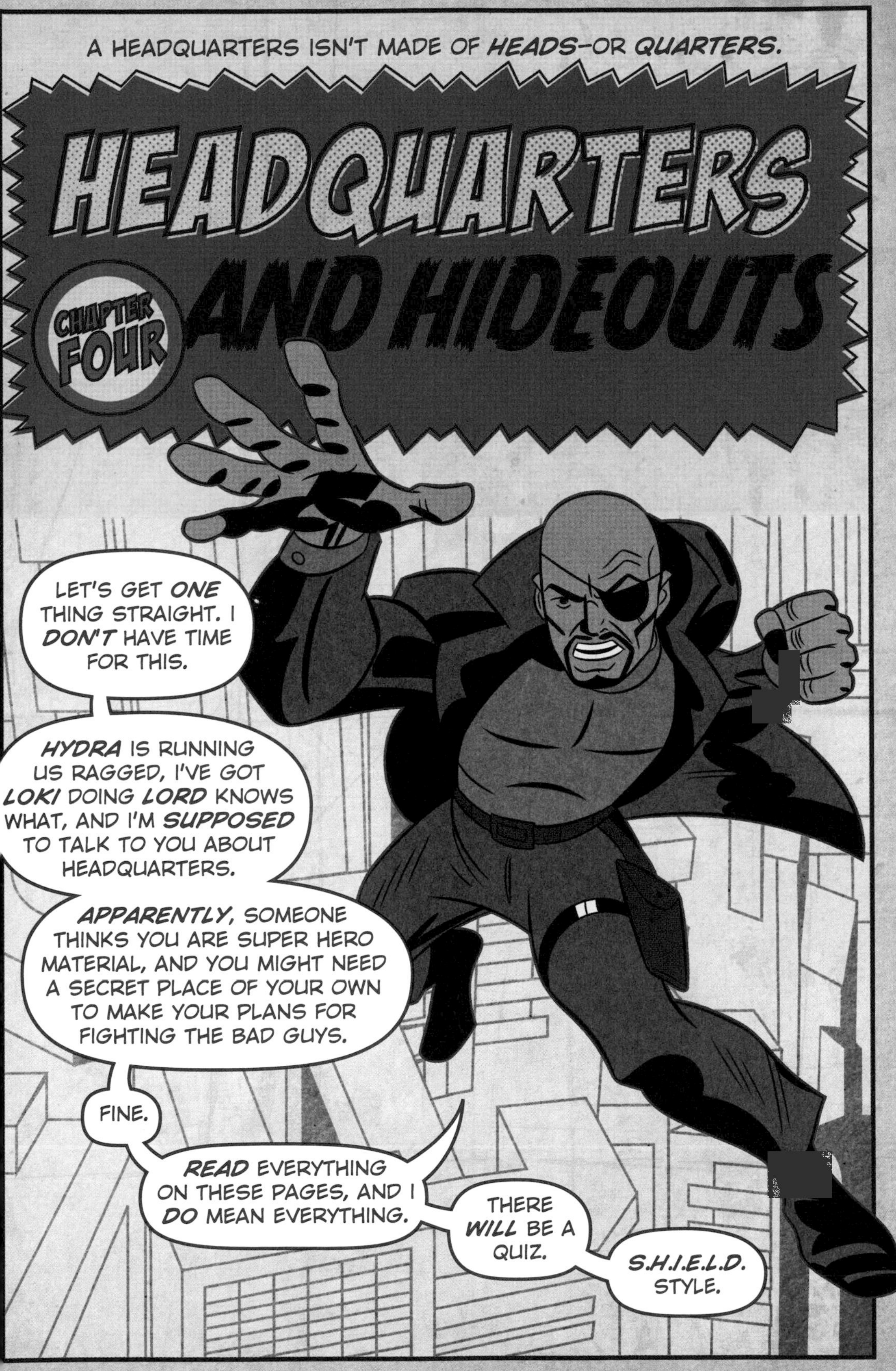
A HEADQUARTERS ISN'T MADE OF HEADS—OR QUARTERS.
CHAPTER FOUR
HEADQUARTERS AND HIDEOUTS
LET'S GET ONE THING STRAIGHT. I DON'T HAVE TIME FOR THIS.
HYDRA IS RUNNING US RAGGED, I'VE GOT LOKI DOING LORD KNOWS WHAT, AND I'M SUPPOSED TO TALK TO YOU ABOUT HEADQUARTERS.
APPARENTLY, SOMEONE THINKS YOU ARE SUPER HERO MATERIAL, AND YOU MIGHT NEED A SECRET PLACE OF YOUR OWN TO MAKE YOUR PLANS FOR FIGHTING THE BAD GUYS.
FINE.
READ EVERYTHING ON THESE PAGES, AND I DO MEAN EVERYTHING.
THERE WILL BE A QUIZ.
S.H.I.E.L.D. STYLE.

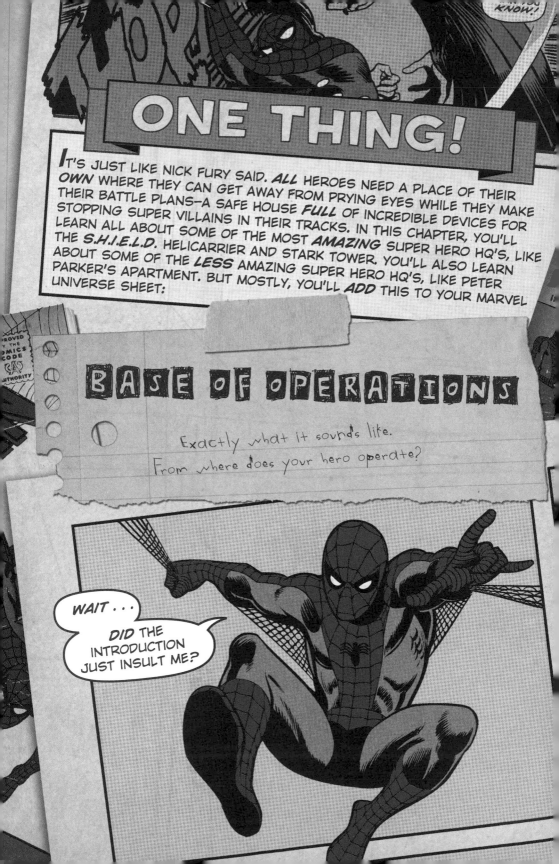

KNOW!

ONE THING!

It's just like Nick Fury said. ALL heroes need a place of their OWN where they can get away from prying eyes while they make their battle plans—a safe house FULL of incredible devices for stopping super villains in their tracks. In this chapter, you'll learn all about some of the most AMAZING super hero HQ's, like the S.H.I.E.L.D. helicarrier and Stark Tower. You'll also learn about some of the LESS amazing super hero HQ's, like Peter Parker's apartment. But mostly, you'll ADD this to your Marvel Universe sheet:

BASE OF OPERATIONS

Exactly what it sounds like.
From where does your hero operate?

WAIT . . .

DID THE INTRODUCTION JUST INSULT ME?

WHETHER YOU BUILD YOUR HERO *HQ* INTO THE SIDE OF A MOUNTAIN OR MAKE A MOBILE BASE OF OPERATIONS LIKE THE *S.H.I.E.L.D.* HELICARRIER, YOU HAVE TO REMEMBER ONE THING ABOUT HEADQUARTERS: *LOCATION, LOCATION, LOCATION.* THAT MAY SOUND LIKE THREE THINGS, BUT IT'S REALLY ONE THING. BUT IT'S AS *IMPORTANT* AS THREE THINGS. *CONFUSED? READ ON!*

LEAST PRACTICAL PLACES TO MAKE YOUR SUPER HERO HEADQUARTERS

10. Shoe box (unless you're Ant-Man or Wasp)

9. Grandma's house

8. Inside bathroom of Red Skull's lair (If you get caught, he'll make you clean it.)

7. In basement of Stark Tower (They have mice.)

6. Neighbor kid's sandbox

5. Clouds (It turns out that clouds aren't solid and you can't walk on them. We found out the hard way.)

4. J. Jonah Jameson's car

3. Inside an active volcano (unless you're Volcano Boy or something)

2. That place by the place with the thing—you know, that thing with the whatsits

1. Tie: busy intersection or factory that makes Hulk's pants

YOU . . .

BUILT . . .

YOUR HEADQUARTERS . . .

IN MY . . .

WHAT?!?

S.H.I.E.L.D. HELICARRIER

PERHAPS THE PRIME EXAMPLE OF A HEADQUARTERS IS *S.H.I.E.L.D.'S* FLYING HELICARRIER. CAPABLE OF CIRCLING THE *GLOBE* CARRYING A VAST ARRAY OF *S.H.I.E.L.D.* AGENTS AND STARK-DESIGNED WEAPONS AND VEHICLES, THE HELICARRIER IS *S.H.I.E.L.D.'S* MOBILE HOME. *BUT* IT'S *NOT* A MOBILE HOME. YOU KNOW WHAT WE MEAN.

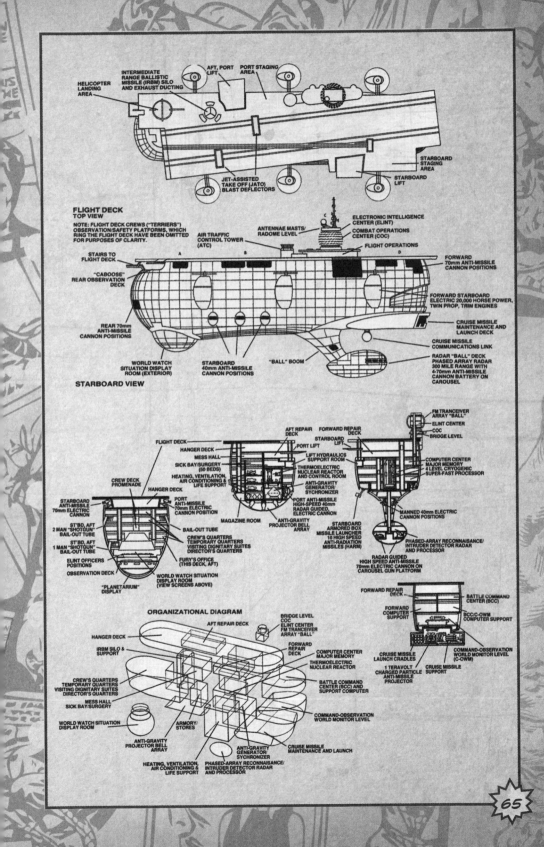

HELICOPTER LANDING AREA

INTERMEDIATE RANGE BALLISTIC MISSILE (IRBM) SILO AND EXHAUST DUCTING

AFT, PORT LIFT

PORT STAGING AREA

STARBOARD STAGING AREA

STARBOARD LIFT

JET-ASSISTED TAKE OFF (JATO) BLAST DEFLECTORS

FLIGHT DECK
TOP VIEW

NOTE: FLIGHT DECK CREWS ("TERRIERS"), OBSERVATION/SAFETY PLATFORMS, WHICH RING THE FLIGHT DECK HAVE BEEN OMITTED FOR PURPOSES OF CLARITY.

AIR TRAFFIC CONTROL TOWER (ATC)

ANTENNAE MASTS/ RADOME LEVEL

ELECTRONIC INTELLIGENCE CENTER (ELINT)

COMBAT OPERATIONS CENTER (COC)

FLIGHT OPERATIONS

STAIRS TO FLIGHT DECK

FORWARD 70mm ANTI-MISSILE CANNON POSITIONS

"CABOOSE" REAR OBSERVATION DECK

FORWARD STARBOARD ELECTRIC 20,000 HORSE POWER, TWIN PROP, TRIM ENGINES

REAR 70mm ANTI-MISSILE CANNON POSITIONS

CRUISE MISSILE MAINTENANCE AND LAUNCH DECK

CRUISE MISSILE COMMUNICATIONS LINK

WORLD WATCH SITUATION DISPLAY ROOM (EXTERIOR)

STARBOARD 40mm ANTI-MISSILE CANNON POSITIONS

"BALL" BOOM

RADAR "BALL" DECK PHASED ARRAY RADAR 300 MILE RANGE WITH 4-70mm ANTI-MISSILE CANNON BATTERY ON CAROUSEL

STARBOARD VIEW

AFT REPAIR DECK

FORWARD REPAIR DECK

FM TRANCEIVER ARRAY "BALL"

ELINT CENTER

COC

BRIDGE LEVEL

FLIGHT DECK

HANGER DECK

MESS HALL

SICK BAY/SURGERY (50 BEDS)

HEATING, VENTILATION, AIR CONDITIONING & LIFE SUPPORT

STARBOARD LIFT

PORT LIFT

LIFT HYDRAULICS SUPPORT ROOM

THERMOELECTRIC NUCLEAR REACTOR AND CONTROL ROOM

ANTI-GRAVITY GENERATOR SYCHRONIZER

COMPUTER CENTER MAJOR MEMORY 4 LEVEL CRYOGENIC SUPER-FAST PROCESSOR

CREW DECK PROMENADE

HANGER DECK

STARBOARD ANTI-MISSILE 70mm ELECTRIC CANNON

PORT ANTI-MISSILE 70mm ELECTRIC CANNON POSITION

PORT ANTI-MISSILE HIGH-SPEED 40mm RADAR GUIDED, ELECTRIC CANNON

MAGAZINE ROOM

ANTI-GRAVITY PROJECTOR BELL ARRAY

MANNED 40mm ELECTRIC CANNON POSITIONS

ST'BD, AFT 2 MAN "SHOTGUN" BAIL-OUT TUBE

BAIL-OUT TUBE

STARBOARD ARMORED BOX MISSILE LAUNCHER 10 HIGH SPEED ANTI-RADIATION MISSILES (HARM)

PHASED-ARRAY RECONNAISANCE/ INTRUDER DETECTOR RADAR AND PROCESSOR

ST'BD, AFT 1 MAN "SHOTGUN" BAIL-OUT TUBE

CREW'S QUARTERS TEMPORARY QUARTERS VISITING DIGNITARY SUITES DIRECTOR'S QUARTERS

ELINT OFFICERS POSITIONS

FURY'S OFFICE (THIS DECK, AFT)

RADAR GUIDED HIGH SPEED ANTI-MISSILE 70mm ELECTRIC CANNON ON CAROUSEL GUN PLATFORM

OBSERVATION DECK

WORLD WATCH SITUATION DISPLAY ROOM (VIEW SCREENS ABOVE)

"PLANETARIUM" DISPLAY

FORWARD REPAIR DECK

FORWARD COMPUTER SUPPORT

BATTLE COMMAND CENTER (BCC)

BCC/C-OWM COMPUTER SUPPORT

ORGANIZATIONAL DIAGRAM

BRIDGE LEVEL COC ELINT CENTER FM TRANCEIVER ARRAY "BALL"

CRUISE MISSILE LAUNCH CRADLES

1 TERAVOLT CHARGED PARTICLE ANTI-MISSILE PROJECTOR

COMMAND-OBSERVATION WORLD MONITOR LEVEL (C-OWM)

CRUISE MISSILE SUPPORT

HANGER DECK

AFT REPAIR DECK

FORWARD REPAIR DECK

IRBM SILO & SUPPORT

COMPUTER CENTER MAJOR MEMORY

THERMOELECTRIC NUCLEAR REACTOR

BATTLE COMMAND CENTER (BCC) AND SUPPORT COMPUTER

CREW'S QUARTERS TEMPORARY QUARTERS VISITING DIGNITARY SUITES DIRECTOR'S QUARTERS

MESS HALL SICK BAY/SURGERY

COMMAND-OBSERVATION WORLD MONITOR LEVEL

WORLD WATCH SITUATION DISPLAY ROOM

ARMORY/ STORES

ANTI-GRAVITY PROJECTOR BELL ARRAY

ANTI-GRAVITY GENERATOR SYCHRONIZER

CRUISE MISSILE MAINTENANCE AND LAUNCH

HEATING, VENTILATION, AIR CONDITIONING & LIFE SUPPORT

PHASED-ARRAY RECONNAISANCE/ INTRUDER DETECTOR RADAR AND PROCESSOR

YOUR HEADQUARTERS *SHOULD* BE SUPER VILLAIN FREE, RIGHT? BUT WHAT HAPPENS IF YOU'RE OUT ON A MISSION AND YOU GO BACK TO YOUR *HQ*, ONLY TO FIND SOMETHING OUT OF PLACE? *WHAT* IF A SNEAKY SUPER VILLAIN (OR LITTLE BROTHER OR SISTER) GOT INSIDE? THERE'S SOMETHING *SIMPLE* YOU CAN DO TO DETECT ANY EVIL INTRUDERS.

WHAT YOU'LL NEED

- A piece of paper
- A pair of scissors
- A healthy snack (you've been reading for a while, you're probably hungry now)

THE SETUP

1. CUT A THIN STRIP OF PAPER (ABOUT THREE INCHES LONG AND ABOUT HALF AN INCH WIDE).

2. PLACE THE PAPER *BENEATH* THE LOWEST DOOR HINGE. IT WILL BE A FEW INCHES ABOVE THE FLOOR

3. CAREFULLY SHUT THE DOOR, MAKING SURE THE PAPER DOESN'T FALL. *YOU* SHOULD BE ABLE TO SEE A SMALL PIECE WHEN THE DOOR IS CLOSED. *LEAVE! EAT* YOUR HEALTHY SNACK, MAYBE.

4. WHEN YOU COME BACK, LOOK AT THE DOOR. IF YOU STILL SEE THE PAPER, *NO* SUPER VILLAIN HAS ENTERED. IF YOU DON'T SEE IT, THAT'S A SURE *SIGN* SOME BAD GUY'S LURKING ABOUT!

FIN

KEEP OUT

MAKE YOUR OWN FLYING HEADQUARTERS

WITH THAT OUT OF THE WAY, HERE'S HOW YOU CAN MAKE YOUR OWN FLYING HEADQUARTERS:

1. *TAKE* A PIECE OF PAPER.

2. *FOLD* IT INTO A PAPER AIRPLANE.

3. *WRITE* THE WORD "HEADQUARTERS" ON IT.

4. *THROW* THAT PLANE. *BOOM!* INSTANT FLYING HEADQUARTERS!

67

AVENGERS MANSION

If you or one of your super hero colleagues is *PRONE* to airsickness, then maybe a helicarrier *ISN'T* for you. You might just prefer something like . . . oh, I don't know, a *MANSION* for your base of operations. There's precedent, too! Before the Avengers moved into Stark Tower, they called stately Avengers Mansion home. *HERE* are the ins and outs of their *HQ*.

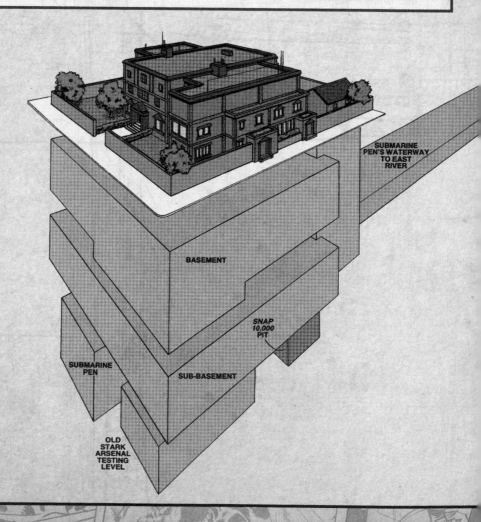

SUBMARINE PEN'S WATERWAY TO EAST RIVER

BASEMENT

SNAP 10,000 PIT

SUBMARINE PEN

SUB-BASEMENT

OLD STARK ARSENAL TESTING LEVEL

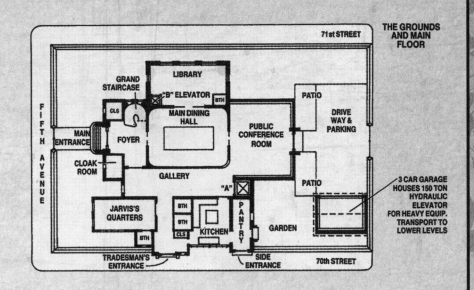

THE GROUNDS AND MAIN FLOOR

71st STREET

LIBRARY

GRAND STAIRCASE

"B" ELEVATOR

BTH

CLS

MAIN DINING HALL

PUBLIC CONFERENCE ROOM

PATIO

DRIVE WAY & PARKING

F I F T H   A V E N U E

MAIN ENTRANCE

FOYER

CLOAK ROOM

GALLERY

"A"

PATIO

JARVIS'S QUARTERS

BTH
BTH
CLS

KITCHEN

P A N T R Y

GARDEN

BTH

TRADESMAN'S ENTRANCE

SIDE ENTRANCE

70th STREET

3 CAR GARAGE HOUSES 150 TON HYDRAULIC ELEVATOR FOR HEAVY EQUIP. TRANSPORT TO LOWER LEVELS

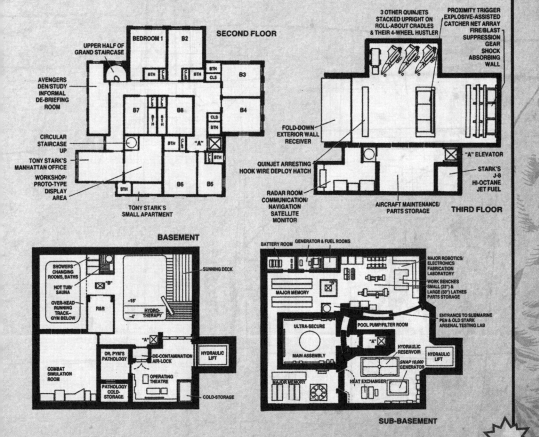

SECOND FLOOR

BEDROOM 1
B2

UPPER HALF OF GRAND STAIRCASE

AVENGERS DEN/STUDY INFORMAL DE-BRIEFING ROOM

BTH
CLS
BTH
CLS

B3

B7
B8
CLS
BTH

B4

CIRCULAR STAIRCASE UP

TONY STARK'S MANHATTAN OFFICE

BTH
"A"

WORKSHOP/ PROTO-TYPE DISPLAY AREA

BTH
B6
B5

TONY STARK'S SMALL APARTMENT

3 OTHER QUINJETS STACKED UPRIGHT ON ROLL-ABOUT CRADLES & THEIR 4-WHEEL HUSTLER

PROXIMITY TRIGGER EXPLOSIVE-ASSISTED CATCHER NET ARRAY FIRE/BLAST SUPPRESSION GEAR SHOCK ABSORBING WALL

FOLD-DOWN EXTERIOR WALL RECEIVER

QUINJET ARRESTING HOOK WIRE DEPLOY HATCH

RADAR ROOM COMMUNICATION/ NAVIGATION SATELLITE MONITOR

AIRCRAFT MAINTENANCE/ PARTS STORAGE

"A" ELEVATOR

STARK'S J-8 HI-OCTANE JET FUEL

THIRD FLOOR

BASEMENT

SHOWERS CHANGING ROOMS, BATHS

"B"

SUNNING DECK

HOT TUB/ SAUNA

OVER-HEAD RUNNING TRACK- GYM BELOW

R&R

HYDRO- THERAPY

-16'
-4'

"A"

DE-CONTAMINATION AIR-LOCK

DR. PYM'S PATHOLOGY

HYDRAULIC LIFT

COMBAT SIMULATION ROOM

PATHOLOGY COLD- STORAGE

OPERATING THEATRE

COLD-STORAGE

BATTERY ROOM

GENERATOR & FUEL ROOMS

MAJOR MEMORY

"B"

MAJOR ROBOTICS/ ELECTRONICS FABRICATION LABORATORY

WORK BENCHES SMALL (22") & LARGE (50") LATHES PARTS STORAGE

ULTRA-SECURE

MAIN ASSEMBLY

POOL PUMP/FILTER ROOM

"A"

ENTRANCE TO SUBMARINE PEN & OLD STARK ARSENAL TESTING LAB

HYDRAULIC RESERVOIR

HYDRAULIC LIFT

MAJOR MEMORY

SNAP 10,000 GENERATOR

HEAT EXCHANGER

SUB-BASEMENT

69

BEFORE *J.A.R.V.I.S.* THE ARTIFICIAL INTELLIGENCE, THERE WAS *EDWIN JARVIS*, THE BUTLER. A *GENTLEMAN'S* GENTLEMAN. THE *HEART* AND *SOUL* OF AVENGERS MANSION, THE MAN WHO KEPT BREAKFAST ON THE TABLE AND THE MASTERS OF EVIL FROM *SOILING* THE CARPETS. YOU'RE GOING TO *NEED* SOMEONE JUST LIKE THAT TO HELP RUN YOUR HEADQUARTERS.

MAKE YOUR OWN JARVIS!

WHAT YOU'LL NEED

- A thin piece of cardboard
- A nontoxic glue stick
- A pair of scissors
- An adult with access to a color copier

© 2016 MARVEL

THE SETUP

1. *ASK* AN ADULT TO MAKE A COLOR COPY OF THIS PAGE. (TRY USING THE WORD *"PLEASE."* IT WORKS WONDERS.)

2. *APPLY* A LAYER OF GLUE TO A PIECE OF THIN CARDBOARD.

3. *PRESS* THE COLOR COPY ONTO THE CARDBOARD AND LET IT DRY.

4. *CUT* OUT THE FIGURE OF JARVIS AND HIS AWESOME VACUUM CLEANER.

5. *BEND* THE TWO TABS AT JARVIS'S FEET, THEN STAND HIM UP.

6. *ASK* HIM FOR TEA AND BISCUITS, AND TO ALERT THE AVENGERS!

FIN

HELICARRIER, MANSION, *COUGH* APARTMENT. HEROES CALL PLENTY OF DIFFERENT PLACES HOME. HERE'S A BRIEF SNAPSHOT OF WHERE SOME SUPER HEROES LIVE.

HERO HANGOUTS

DOCTOR STRANGE	177A Bleecker Street, Greenwich Village, New York, New York
HULK	Caves across the United States (contiguous states only)
IRON FIST	Mystic city of K'un Lun
STAR-LORD	Spaceship Milano
THOR	Asgard
MAN-THING	The Nexus of All Realities, which is a fancy way of saying a big swamp in Florida

WHATEVER KNOWS *SARCASM* BURNS AT THE MAN-THING'S TOUCH!

PETER PARKER'S PAD

WE'RE NOT SAYING THAT HAVING YOUR HEADQUARTERS INSIDE AN APARTMENT IS *LAME. NOT* AT ALL. *WHAT* WE'RE SAYING IS, HAVING YOUR HEADQUARTERS INSIDE PETER PARKER'S APARTMENT *IS* LAME.

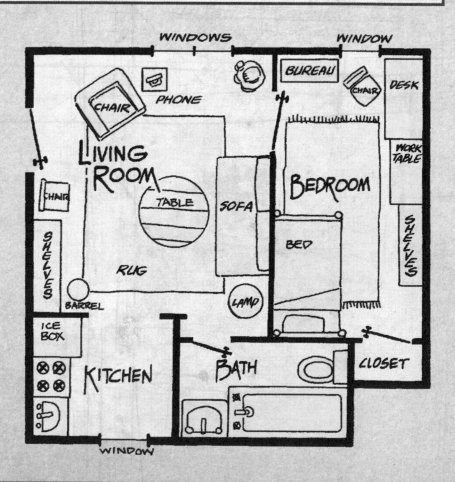

EVERY DAY IN EVERY WAY I AM GETTING BETTER AND BETTER!
BURMA SHAVE
STAR WARS

DON'T ASK US WHY, BUT HEROES AND VILLAINS BOTH LIKE TO NAME THEIR HEADQUARTERS. IT'S A LITTLE *STRANGE*. AFTER ALL, YOU DON'T HAVE A NAME FOR YOUR HOME, *DO YOU?** SEE IF YOU CAN TELL, JUST BY LOOKING AT THESE NAMES, IF THE LAIR BELONGS TO A *HERO* OR A *VILLAIN*.

BY ANY OTHER NAME . . .

HYDRO-BASE
HERO ☐
VILLAIN ☐

THE GOBLIN HOUSE
HERO ☐
VILLAIN ☐

SANCTUM SANCTORUM
HERO ☐
VILLAIN ☐

SERPENT CITADEL
HERO ☐
VILLAIN ☐

ANSWERS:
1) H (Avengers), 2) V (Green Goblin), 3) H (Doctor Strange), 4) V (Serpent Society)

DID YOU KNOW?

DID YOU KNOW THAT ANT-MAN ONCE HAD HIS VERY *OWN* HEADQUARTERS? AND *NO*, IT WASN'T INSIDE AN ANT HILL, *SMARTY-PANTS*. IT WAS A TEENY ANT-SIZED LAIR BUILT INTO A REGULAR OL' HOUSE!

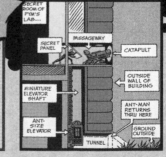

SECRET ROOM OF PYM'S LAB...
SECRET PANEL
PASSAGEWAY
CATAPULT
OUTSIDE WALL OF BUILDING
MINIATURE ELEVATOR SHAFT
ANT-MAN RETURNS THRU HERE
ANT-SIZE ELEVATOR
TUNNEL
GROUND OUTSIDE

*IF YOU DO, PLEASE TELL US YOU CALL IT *LARRY*. LARRY IS A GOOD NAME.

THE **MOST** IMPORTANT FEATURE OF ANY HEADQUARTERS OR HIDEOUT IS THE **SELF-DESTRUCT** SWITCH. YOU **NEVER** KNOW WHEN YOU'LL HAVE TO KEEP ALL YOUR SUPER HERO SECRETS OUT OF THE MULTIPLE HANDS OF **DOCTOR OCTOPUS**. WHILE THERE ARE LAWS AGAINST OUR INCLUDING AN **ACTUAL** SELF-DESTRUCT SWITCH IN THIS BOOK, NOTHING SAYS WE CAN'T GIVE YOU A **FAKE** SELF-DESTRUCT LABEL TO PLACE OVER ANY ORDINARY LIGHT SWITCH IN YOUR HOME.

READ THE DESTRUCTIONS

WHAT YOU'LL NEED

- A pair of scissors

- Transparent tape

- An adult with access to a color copier

THE SETUP

1. ASK AN ADULT TO MAKE A **COLOR COPY** OF THIS PAGE.

2. **CUT OUT** THE SELF-DESTRUCT SWITCH ON THE DOTTED LINES. MAKE SURE YOU **CUT OUT** THE SPACE INDICATED FOR THE SWITCH, TOO.

3. NOW **TAPE** THIS PIECE OVER AN ORDINARY LIGHT SWITCH.

4. **WAIT** UNTIL YOUR FAMILY FILLS THE ROOM. CASUALLY POINT OUT THE SWITCH, THEN FLIP IT!

5. **HILARITY** ENSUES.

FIN

LIKE HEIMDALL, YOU'RE GUARDING THE BIFROST OF YOUR IMAGINATION, JUST WAITING TO UNLEASH IT TO TRANSPORT YOUR HEADQUARTERS IDEAS FROM YOUR BRAIN TO REALITY! THAT WAS A *VERY* TORTURED ANALOGY. BUT YOU GET THE *POINT*. IT'S TIME TO TAKE *EVERYTHING* YOU LEARNED IN THIS CHAPTER TO DECIDE ON YOUR VERY *OWN* BASE!

ALL ABOUT THAT BASE

HERE'S WHAT YOU DO:
GRAB THE ATTRIBUTE AND NUMBER DICE. THEY HAVEN'T SEEN YOU IN A WHILE, SO BE SURE TO LET THEM KNOW IT'S NOTHING PERSONAL. *ROLL* EACH OF THE DICE, THEN FIND THE ICON AND NUMBER YOU ROLLED ON THE NEXT PAGE. *PUT* THE TWO PHRASES TOGETHER. *CONGRATULATIONS,* YOU NOW HAVE YOUR HEADQUARTERS! *WRITE* DOWN THIS INFORMATION UNDER *"BASE OF OPERATIONS"* ON THE MARVEL UNIVERSE SHEET ON PAGE 166. (PSSST! YOU CAN COME UP WITH YOUR OWN IDEA IF YOU WANT!)

YOU CAN ALSO WRITE IN YOUR *OWN* LOCATIONS USING THE *BLANK* SPACES!

1 ATTRIBUTES!

1. INTELLIGENCE
CASTLE

2. STRENGTH
WAREHOUSE

3. SPEED
SKYSCRAPER

4. DURABILITY
OLD REFRIGERATOR

5. ENERGY PROJECTION
WASHINGTON MONUMENT

6. FIGHTING
MOON

2 SPECIAL POWERS!

BASEMENT

CLOSET

STRONGHOLD

SATELLITE

OBSERVATORY

FISH TANK

77

Now that you've **SETTLED** on your secret lair, it's time to design it. If you're based in a moon closet, what does that look like? If you're **KICKIN'** it in a warehouse stronghold, what **DEFENSES** does it have? These are **ALL** questions you'll need to answer as you **DRAW** up the floor plans for your hero headquarters!

MARVELOUS MAKE

WHAT YOU'LL NEED

- A pencil with an eraser

SPECIAL FEATURES

GETTING STARTED:

1. **WRITE** THE NAME OF YOUR BASE OF OPERATIONS IN THE SPACE PROVIDED ON PAGE 79.

2. IN THE SPECIAL FEATURES BOXES, **WRITE** SOME OF THE COOL FEATURES YOUR BASE WILL HAVE. IF YOU NEED SOME INSPIRATION, CHECK OUT THE BRAINSTORM BOX.

3. **DRAW** OUT THE FLOOR PLAN OF YOUR HEADQUARTERS ON THE GRID!

WEAPONS:

DEFENSES:

SECURITY SYSTEMS:

BRAINSTORM BOX!
Stuff you can include:
- Intruder alert!
- Alien detector!
- Negative Zone Access Port!
- Extra refrigerator for pie!
- Freakishly long hallway to nowhere!
- Bottomless pit!
- Swimming pool!

HEADQUARTERS NAME:

CHECK YOURSELF

1 What's the least practical place to make your Super Hero headquarters? *Tile*

| FACTORY THAT MAKES HULK'S PANTS | OR | BUSY INTERSECTION |

2 What's the least practical name for your Super Hero headquarters? *Red Skull Half Bath*

 | OR | RED SKULL'S HALF BATH

3 Who was the Avengers' butler? *Edwin Jarvis*

 | OR |

4 If you found yourself in the Nexus of All Realities, which hero would you meet? *Man-Thing*

 | OR |

5 We don't want to make him feel worse, but Peter Parker's apartment is a terrible hideout. *None*

| AGREE | OR | STRONGLY AGREE |

ANSWERS: 1) Trick question; this was a tie, remember? 2) Red Skull's Half Bath, 3) Edwin Jarvis, 4) Man-Thing, 5) This wasn't really a question; we just wanted to bring it up again. If you got all the answers correct, you should ask a parent or guardian for cake, which is much better than pie.

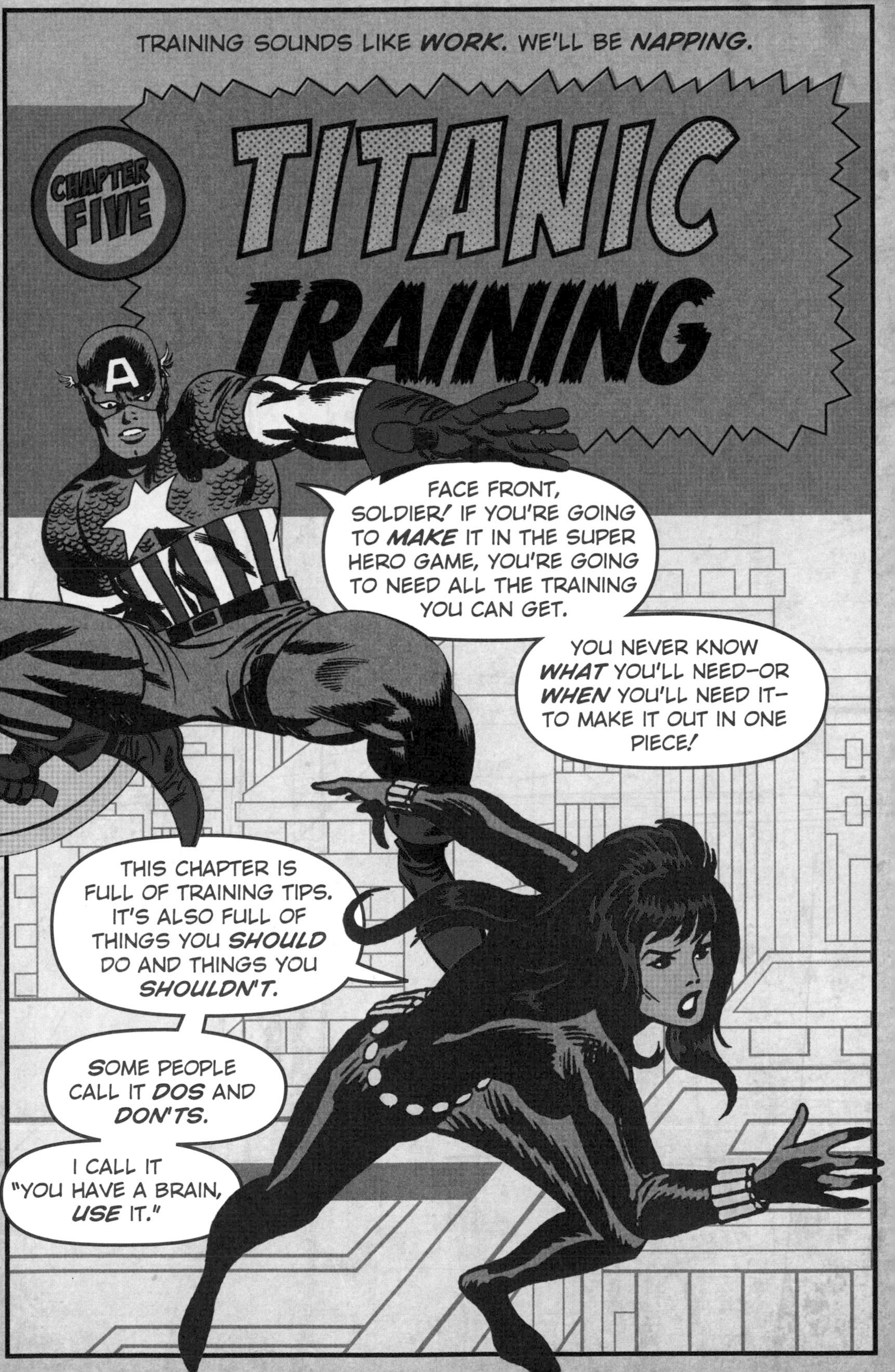
TRAINING SOUNDS LIKE WORK. WE'LL BE NAPPING.
CHAPTER FIVE
TITANIC TRAINING
FACE FRONT, SOLDIER! IF YOU'RE GOING TO MAKE IT IN THE SUPER HERO GAME, YOU'RE GOING TO NEED ALL THE TRAINING YOU CAN GET.
YOU NEVER KNOW WHAT YOU'LL NEED–OR WHEN YOU'LL NEED IT–TO MAKE IT OUT IN ONE PIECE!
THIS CHAPTER IS FULL OF TRAINING TIPS. IT'S ALSO FULL OF THINGS YOU SHOULD DO AND THINGS YOU SHOULDN'T.
SOME PEOPLE CALL IT DOS AND DON'TS.
I CALL IT "YOU HAVE A BRAIN, USE IT."

ONE THING!

JUST BECAUSE CAPTAIN AMERICA AND BLACK WIDOW SAID THAT TRAINING AND *DOS* AND *DON'TS* ARE IMPORTANT DOESN'T MEAN YOU SHOULD *BELIEVE* IT. THAT'S A *LIE.* OF COURSE IT MEANS YOU *SHOULD* BELIEVE IT. YOU SHOULD BELIEVE IT A *LOT!* THOSE TWO ARE THE *EXPERTS.* THEY'VE SURVIVED THIS LONG BECAUSE THEY KNOW THE *RIGHT* THINGS TO DO. THEY TRAIN *HARD.* THEY DON'T BRING SQUIRT GUNS TO A SUPER VILLAIN FIGHT.

THINGS THAT YOU'VE TRAINED TO DO!

YOU'VE BOTH BEEN GETTING 'TLESS-- YOU COULD *USE* A 'LE ACTION! SO, TRY TO FIND HIM IF YOU WISH!

I'LL STAY AND MIND THE STORE!

VERY WELL! COME, PIETRO--!

MOMENTS LATER, CAP RETURNS TO HIS TRAINING ROUTINE...

SINCE I POSSESS NO SPECIAL, NATURAL POWERS LIKE THE OTHERS, I MUST NEVER STOP TRAINING!

ALSO, IT KEEPS MY MIND OFF THE FACT THAT *NICK FURY* HAS NEVER ANSWERED THE LETTER I SENT HIM!

WHY HASN'T HE *ANSWERED* ME? WHY THE UNBEARABLE *DELAY?* *NOBODY* CAN BE BETTER QUALIFIED FOR THE JOB THAN *I!!*

*F*OR THE *ULTIMATE* IN TRAINING TIPS, WE TURNED TO SOMEONE WHO TRAINS *A LOT* AND SOMEONE WHO TRAINS *LESS* THAN A LOT, WHICH IS TO SAY *NOT AT ALL.* TAKE A LOOK AT THESE TOP TRAINING TIPS, AND YOU'LL BECOME A PERSON WHO HAS READ THEM*!*

TRAINING TIPS FROM CAPTAIN AMERICA AND HULK

10. Use your opponent's force against them.

9. Stay crouched in a fight. It'll keep your center of gravity lower, making you harder to push around.

8. Smash puny human.

7. Swim. It's great exercise and fun, too!

6. Smash puny army.

5. Warm up by stretching before you start a training session.

4. Never stop reading. A keen mind is required to be a Super Hero!

3. Eat beans. Hulk like beans.

2. Stop, drop, and roll. Three words to live by!

1. Tie: keep your shield close to your body/ **SMASH!!!**

AVOID GETTING HIT BY A DEATH RAY!

YOU'RE GOING TO FIND YOURSELF DIVING *A LOT.* JUST PUTTING IT OUT THERE. WHEN YOU'RE A SUPER HERO, PEOPLE (*BAD PEOPLE*) ARE CONSTANTLY *SHOOTING* THINGS AT YOU. ENERGY BLASTERS, KINETIC WEAPONS, DEATH RAYS (SEE *FIGURE A*)—*ESPECIALLY* DEATH RAYS. HERE YOU'LL FIND THREE *FOOLPROOF* METHODS FOR GIVING THE DEATH RAY THE SLIP.

FIGURE A: DEATH RAY. DO NOT GET HIT BY THIS.

METHOD 1:

"HEY, WHAT'S THAT?"

Favored by Super Heroes for decades, this method relies on the Super Villain's gullibility. What you have to do:

1. Just before the Super Villain's about to shoot you with a death ray, act surprised.

2. Point over the villain's shoulder and say, "Hey, what's that?" Variations include, "Look! Behind you!" and "There's a Frankenstein's Monster right next to you!"*

3. While the Super Villain is distracted by your expert ruse, stop them. Slightly less brave Super Heroes may take this opportunity to run away.

FIGURE B: A FRANKENSTEIN'S MONSTER

*IF THERE REALLY IS A FRANKENSTEIN'S MONSTER NEXT TO THEM, YOU WON'T NEED TO SAY THIS. SEE *FIGURE B.*

METHOD 2:

DON'T BE THERE.

Sounds easy, right? This one requires you to actually move. You could try:

1. Jumping. This seems to be the preferred way to avoid getting caught by a death ray blast.

2. Falling down. It's less elegant, but it gets the job done.

3. Jumping, then falling down. This has the added benefit of confusing your enemy, because why would you do both?

METHOD 3:

TIME TRAVEL.

This one's slightly more complex but surprisingly effective.

1. Before starting your fight, travel forward in time to the fortieth century. Find Kang (see figure C), and "borrow" fortieth-century technology.

2. Travel back in time to the precise moment when the bad guy's about to shoot.

3. Use fortieth-century device to defeat Super Villain.

4. Alert readers may ask, "If you had a time machine, why not travel back in time and avoid getting shot by the death ray altogether?" If you're so smart, why don't you write this book?

FIGURE C: KANG. NOTE STYLISH PANTS/SOCKS COMBO.

STAY FROSTY

WHILE WE CAN'T POSSIBLY PROVIDE EVERY SINGLE DO AND DON'T (WE WOULD NEED AT LEAST ANOTHER PAGE FOR THAT, AND LET'S BE HONEST, PAPER DOESN'T GROW ON TREES*), WE HAVE ASKED AN ASSORTMENT OF SUPER HEROES TO PROVIDE ONE OF EACH.

DO WASH YOUR COSTUME REGULARLY.

DON'T FORGET TO ASK YOUR DOCTOR IF HE OR SHE MIGHT BE MYSTERIO IN DISGUISE.

DO KEEP YOUR WEAPONS IN GOOD WORKING ORDER.

DON'T TRUST ANYONE WHO SAYS *"TRUST ME."*

DO TAKE INSPIRATION FROM YOUR FAVORITE HEROES!

DON'T BE NEGATIVE! (MAYBE THAT SHOULD BE *"DO BE POSITIVE"!*)

DO MAKE GOOD FRIENDS WHEREVER YOU CAN.

DON'T FIGHT ANYONE WITH SILVER WEAPONS, BECAUSE *OW.*

DO GOOD.

DON'T DON'T DO GOOD.

I AM GROOT.

I AM GROOT.

86

*YOU MAY THINK IT DOES, BUT REST ASSURED, IT DOESN'T.

DO AIM TWICE, FIRE ONCE.

DON'T TAKE IT PERSONALLY WHEN THEY CALL YOU *HAWK GUY*.

. . .

. . .

DO USE YOUR POWERS WISELY.

DON'T GET YOUR HAIR CUT UNLESS YOU ABSOLUTELY HAVE TO.

DO MAKE TECHNOLOGY WORK FOR YOU.

DON'T MAKE AN ARTIFICIAL INTELLIGENCE THAT COULD DESTROY THE WORLD.

DO KEEP BOTH FEET ON THE GROUND, EVEN WHEN YOU'RE FLYING.

DON'T RELY ON YOUR GADGETS ONLY.

DO STAY ALERT AND BE READY FOR ANYTHING.

DON'T FORGET WHO YOU ARE AND WHAT YOU STAND FOR.

DO LEARN AS MUCH AS YOU CAN.

DON'T TEASE THE MINDLESS ONES.

DO HONOR THY NAME AND THY FAMILY.

DO NOT HEED THOSE WHO FIND HUMOR IN CALLING THE BIFROST A *RAINBOW BRIDGE*.

DO GET OUT THERE AND MAKE A DIFFERENCE!

DON'T WORRY ABOUT ANYONE CALLING YOU *PIG HEAD*.

87

RICOCHET!

HAVE WE GOT A TRAINING EXERCISE FOR YOU! *HELP* BLACK WIDOW AND CAPTAIN AMERICA TAKE OUT AS MANY *HYDRA AGENTS* AS POSSIBLE. BUT MAKE SURE YOU DON'T CLOCK ANY *S.H.I.E.L.D. AGENTS* ALONG THE WAY!

THE RULES!

1. **Grab** a pencil. Teach it who's boss.

2. **Place** the tip of your pencil on either Captain America **or** Black Widow.

3. Take a good **look** at the page, making note of where the Hydra and S.H.I.E.L.D. agents are **located**.

4. **Close** your eyes. **No** peeking! If you peek, we'll know.

5. Now **draw** a line from one side of the page to the other. **Cross** out as many Hydra agents as you can from memory while missing the S.H.I.E.L.D. agents.

6. **Check** the scoring section to see how you did!

SCORING!

Count how many Hydra agents you drew a line through. Then subtract the number of S.H.I.E.L.D. agents you hit.

0-3 Hydra agents: Better luck next time.

4-5 Hydra agents: Maybe Cap will let you carry his shield. . . .

6-7 Hydra agents: You've got **"sidekick"** written all over you!

8-9 Hydra agents: Hello, hero!

10-11 Hydra agents: You **peeked,** didn't you?

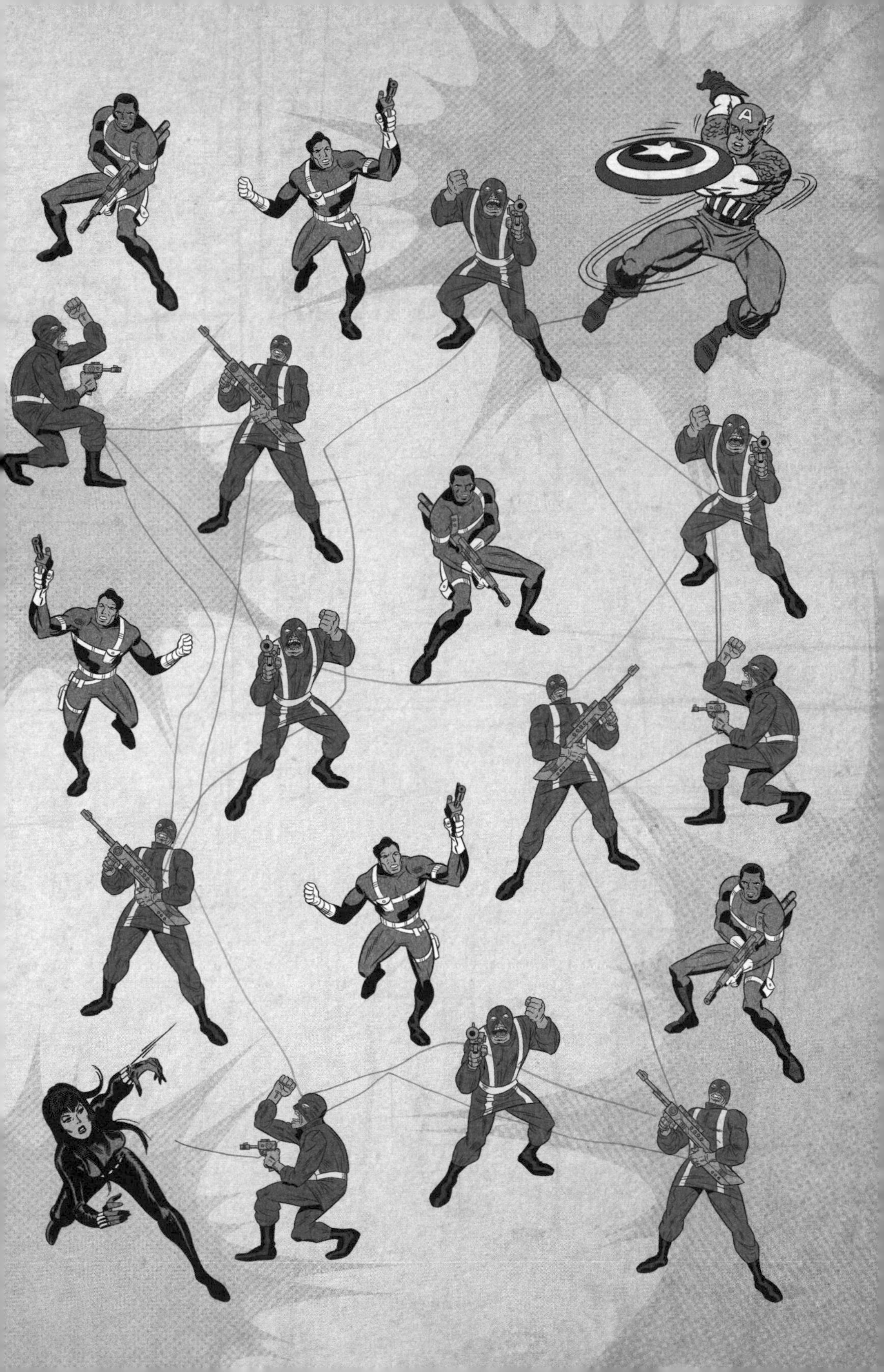

PRECIOUS METALS ARE *VERY* HARD TO COME BY. THAT'S WHAT MAKES THEM SO *PRECIOUS!* THAT AND THEY'RE *CUTE.* THAT SAID, THERE'S NO METAL MORE DIFFICULT TO COME ACROSS THAN *VIBRANIUM—* THE WAKANDAN METAL THAT MAKES CAPTAIN AMERICA'S SHIELD SO *AMAZING.* WHILE WE CAN'T HELP YOU MAKE A VIBRANIUM-ALLOY SHIELD, WE CAN SHOW YOU HOW TO MAKE A SHIELD OF YOUR VERY OWN.

MAKE YOUR OWN SHIELD!

NO MATTER HOW MANY TIMES YOU'VE ASKED HIM TO BORROW IT, CAPTAIN AMERICA TELLS YOU HE'S STILL USING HIS SHIELD. IF HE WANTS TO BE THAT WAY, *FINE. GO AHEAD* AND MAKE YOUR OWN! WHO *NEEDS* VIBRANIUM WHEN YOU HAVE . . . *ULTRA-ALUMINUM?!?*

WHAT YOU'LL NEED

- A sturdy piece of cardboard
- Aluminum foil (which we'll call Ultra-Aluminum from here out; it sounds cooler)
- Duct tape (see page 37)
- An old sock (sounds attractive when said like that)
- A pair of scissors
- Permanent markers

THE SETUP

TAKE THE CARDBOARD AND YOUR SCISSORS. *DECIDE* THE SHAPE YOU WANT YOUR SHIELD TO HAVE, THEN CUT THAT SHAPE FROM THE CARDBOARD.

CAREFULLY COVER YOUR SHIELD SHAPE WITH *ULTRA-ALUMINUM*, POSSIBLY THE MOST PRECIOUS METAL EVER. *IT'S SO* PRECIOUS THAT YOU *CAN COOK FOOD ON IT.*

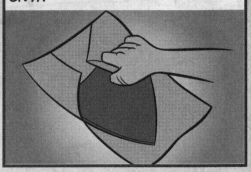

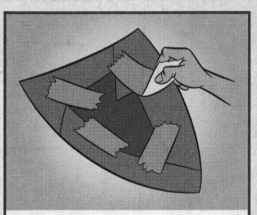

USE THE DUCT TAPE TO SECURE THE *ULTRA-ALUMINUM* IN PLACE.

AGAIN, USING THE DUCT-TAPE-AS-MEANS-TO-SECURE-THINGS SYSTEM, SECURE THAT OLD SOCK TO THE BACK OF THE SHIELD. *THIS* WILL BE THE HANDLE THROUGH WHICH YOU CAN SLING YOUR ARM.

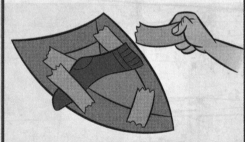

DECIDE ON THE DESIGN OF YOUR SHIELD, THEN USE THE PERMANENT MARKERS TO DECORATE IT.

FIGHT EVIL! OR YOUR SIBLINGS! PROBABLY THE SAME THING!

YOU *TRAIN*, YOU *TRAIN*, AND YOU *TRAIN* SOME MORE. YOU'RE READY TO GO UP AGAINST THE BAD GUYS USING YOUR SPECIAL SKILLS. WHICH ARE . . . WHAT, EXACTLY? HERE'S WHERE YOU'LL *DISCOVER* YOUR CHARACTER'S SPECIAL TALENTS.

IT'S ALL IN THE REFLEXES

HERE'S WHAT YOU DO: *TAKE* THE ATTRIBUTE AND NUMBER DICE. *ROLL* THE DICE, MAKING NOTE OF THE ICON AND NUMBER THAT COME UP. *FIND* THEM IN THE CHART ON PAGE 93. *TAKE* YOUR TWO SPECIAL TALENTS AND WRITE THEM IN THE SPACE PROVIDED ON THE MARVEL UNIVERSE SHEET, PAGE 165. IF YOU'RE FEELING ADVENTUROUS—AND SINCE YOU'RE LEARNING TO BECOME A SUPER HERO, *OF COURSE YOU'RE FEELING ADVENTUROUS*—YOU CAN ALSO WRITE IN A SPECIAL SKILL OF YOUR OWN CREATION!

YOU CAN ALSO WRITE IN YOUR *OWN* POWERS USING THE *SKILLS* SPACES!

1 ATTRIBUTES!

1. INTELLIGENCE
UNDERWATER
TRACKING

2. STRENGTH
GHOST
COMMUNICATION

3. SPEED
MEAT VISION

4. DURABILITY
ABILITY TO STUB
OTHER PEOPLE'S
TOES

5. ENERGY PROJECTION
HYPNOSIS

6. FIGHTING
UNBREAKABLE
ELBOWS

2 SPECIAL POWERS!

RADIOACTIVE EAR
BLASTS

HAIR THAT LOOKS
LIKE A WIG
(BUT ISN'T)

SUPERIOR GIZMO

HUMAN LIE
DETECTOR

POWER TO SMELL
EVIL WITHIN A
300-METER RADIUS

INSTANT RECALL OF
SEEMINGLY USELESS
TRIVIA

It's one of those things that you hope *DOESN'T* happen, but invariably, it *DOES*. The bad guys up and decide to drop an *ENTIRE* mountain on top of you and your super hero buddies. If this doesn't make your web-shooters weep, we don't know what will. *LUCKY* for you, the Hulk has some helpful hints that will prove *USEFUL* in exactly such a situation.

HOLD AN ENTIRE MOUNTAIN OVER YOUR HEAD

STEP 1: HULK SAYS DON'T PANIC. JUST BECAUSE ENTIRE MOUNTAIN DROPPED ON YOUR HEAD, NO REASON TO PANIC.

STEP 2: HULK SAYS USE SUPER STRENGTH. IF YOU SUPER STRONG, THAT GOOD. GO TO STEP 4. IF NOT, GO TO STEP 3.

STEP 3: PANIC.

STEP 4: HOLD UP ENTIRE MOUNTAIN. THIS MAY SOUND HARD, BUT IT NOT. JUST LIKE HOLDING UP A ROCK, IF ROCK WAS A MOUNTAIN.

STEP 5: SMASH MOUNTAIN.

STEP 6: REPEAT STEP 5 UNTIL MOUNTAIN GONE.

STEP 7: EAT BEST FOOD EVER, BEANS.

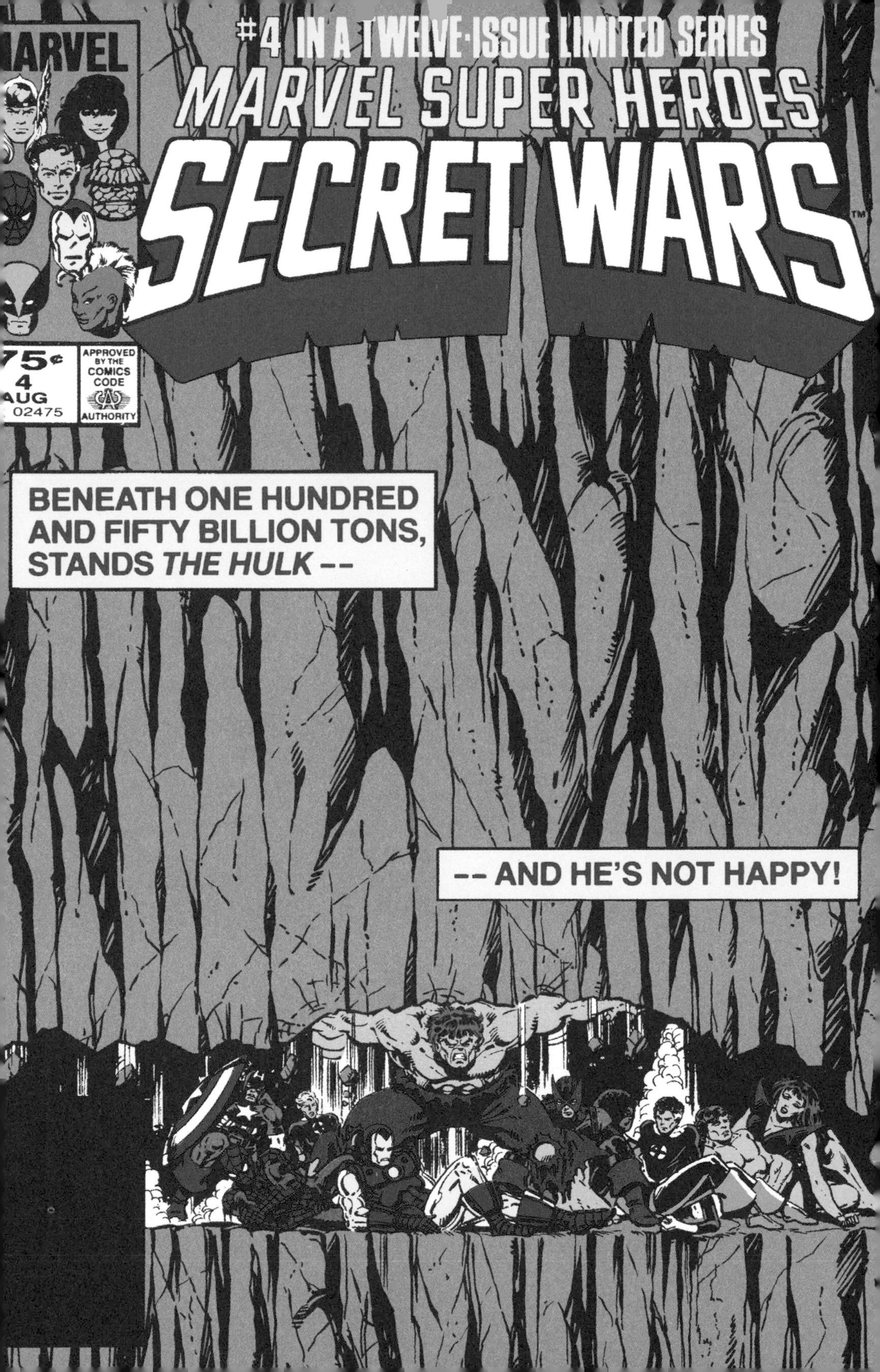
MARVEL
#4 IN A TWELVE-ISSUE LIMITED SERIES
MARVEL SUPER HEROES
SECRET WARS™
75¢
4
AUG
02475
APPROVED BY THE COMICS CODE AUTHORITY
BENEATH ONE HUNDRED AND FIFTY BILLION TONS, STANDS THE HULK --
-- AND HE'S NOT HAPPY!

*T*RAINING IS NECESSARY FOR ANY SOLDIER. THAT GOES FOR SUPER HEROES, TOO! HERE ARE SOME *SIMPLE* THINGS YOU CAN DO RIGHT AT HOME THAT WILL HELP YOU GET READY TO FIGHT THE FORCES OF EVIL.

SHIPSHAPE, SOLDIER!

STAY ACTIVE!

Keep your body moving for at least one hour each day—even if you're just walking up and down stairs (pretend each step is Red Skull's face and you're dancing the Lindy on it)!

DRINK WATER!

It's important to stay hydrated throughout the day. Water's just the ticket . . . even if Hawkeye tries to convince you that coffee's better.

STRETCH!

It's important to stretch out before you exercise. It will keep your body limber and help reduce injuries.

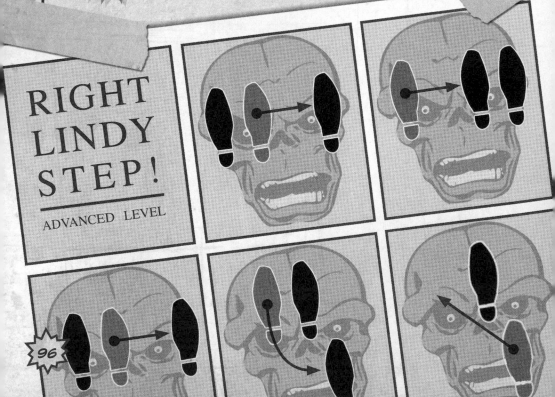

RIGHT LINDY STEP!

ADVANCED LEVEL

HE'S NO SUPER HERO, BUT THAT DOESN'T MEAN THAT *DAILY BUGLE* PUBLISHER J. JONAH JAMESON *DOESN'T* HAVE A THING OR *TEN* TO SAY ABOUT *DON'TS!*

DON'TS FROM J. JONAH JAMESON

10. Don't tell me Spider-Man is a hero.

9. Don't tell me Spider-Man is anything but a masked menace!

8. Don't bring me pictures showing Spider-Man doing anything good.

7. Don't put starch in my pants.

6. Don't tell Peter Parker he's a really good photographer.

5. Don't tell anyone where I keep the really good chocolate.

4. Don't smile, unless you smile when you're insulting Spider-Man.

3. Don't ever get hooked up to a bomb with Spider-Man.

2. Don't let your astronaut son turn into a Man-Wolf who has to be saved by Spider-Man.

1. Just don't.

YOU'VE HEARD FROM THE HEROES. NOW IT'S TIME TO *HEAR* FROM YOU! YOU'VE BEEN TRAINING, AND BY NOW YOU'VE DISCOVERED SOME THINGS THAT WORK FOR YOU (AND SOME THAT *DON'T*). KEEP TRACK OF THEM HERE!

MAKE YOUR OWN DOS AND DON'TS!

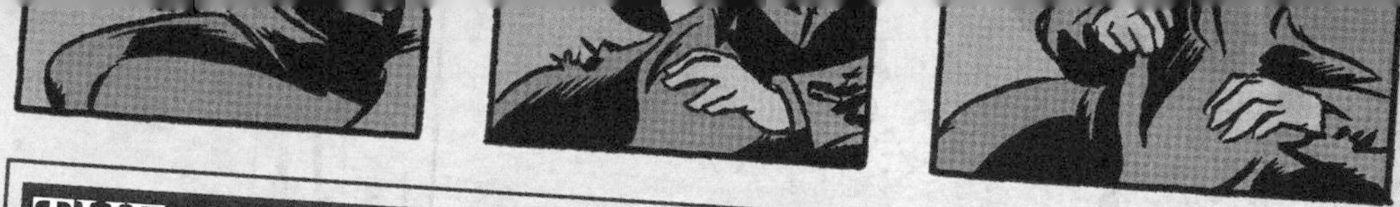

THE OFFICIAL DO AND DON'T LIST OF:

____

(Your Super Hero name here)

DO	DON'T

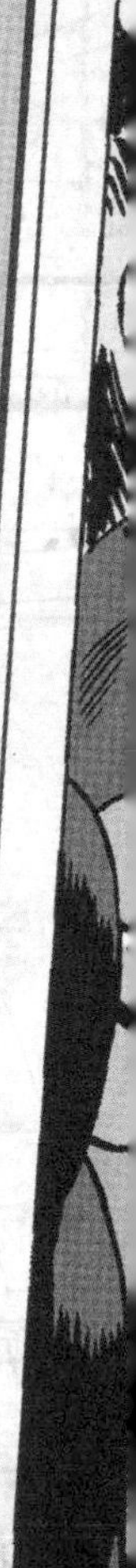

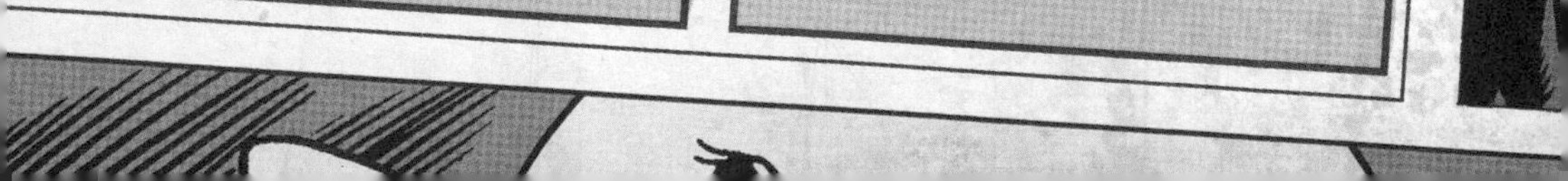

DON'T WAIT ANOTHER SECOND! **DO** ANSWER THESE QUESTIONS AND SEE HOW MUCH YOU **LEARNED** IN THIS CHAPTER!

DO . . . TAKE THIS TEST!

1 When trapped under a mountain, it might be helpful to be:
→ STRONG OR ABLE TO NOT BE TRAPPED UNDER A MOUNTAIN

2 Which hero is **NOT** Groot?
→  OR

3 Which Super Villain sports a fancy slacks/socks combo?
→  OR

4 Ultra-Aluminum is stronger than Vibranium.
→ TRUE OR FALSE

5 Do you think the Hulk would work for beans?
→ SEEMS LIKE HE WOULD OR NOT A CHANCE

ANSWERS:
1) Strong, 2) Chameleon disguised as Groot, 3) Kang the Conqueror, 4) Seriously? 5) Seems like he would.

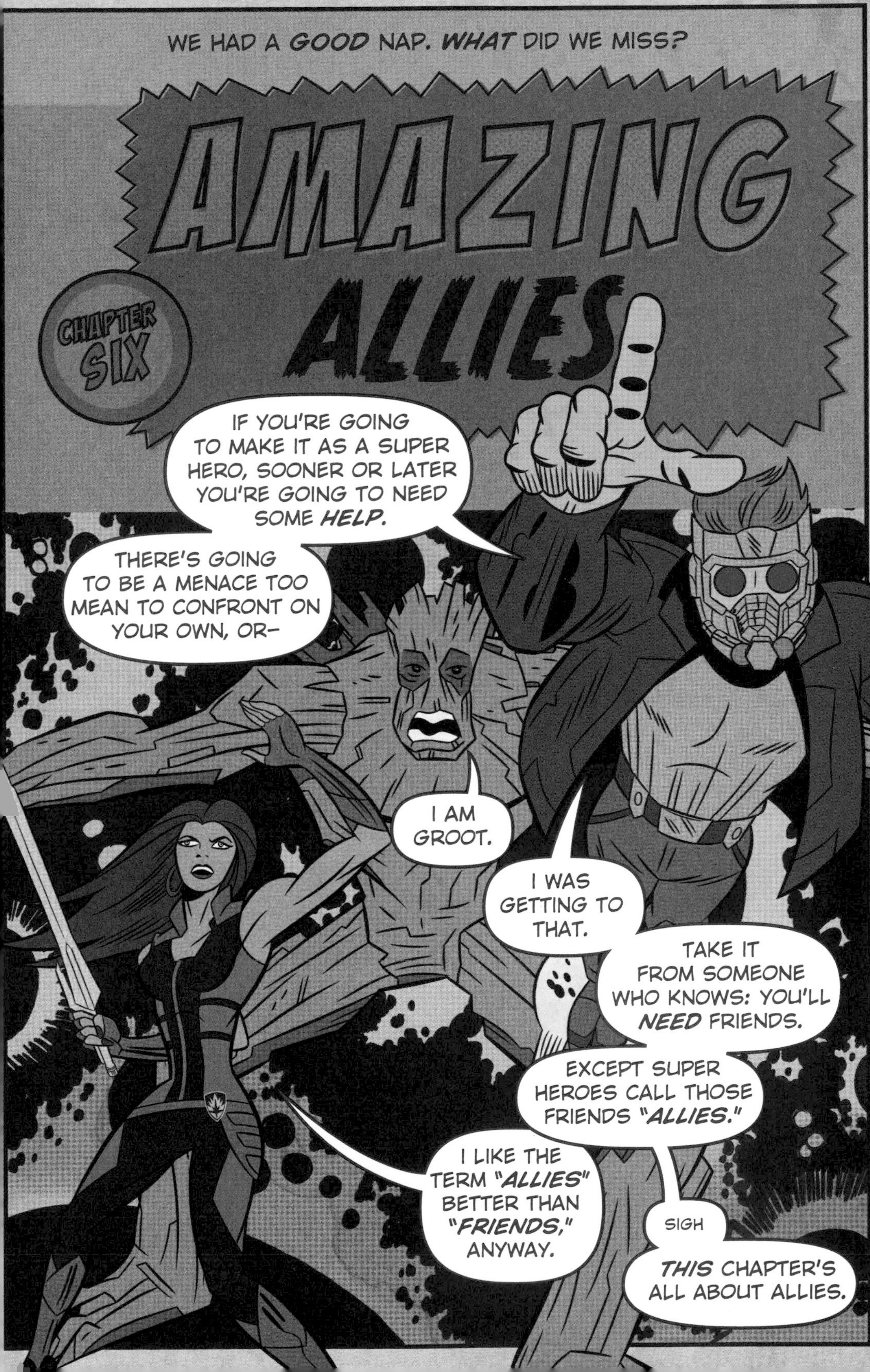
WE HAD A GOOD NAP. WHAT DID WE MISS?
AMAZING ALLIES
CHAPTER SIX
IF YOU'RE GOING TO MAKE IT AS A SUPER HERO, SOONER OR LATER YOU'RE GOING TO NEED SOME HELP.
THERE'S GOING TO BE A MENACE TOO MEAN TO CONFRONT ON YOUR OWN, OR–
I AM GROOT.
I WAS GETTING TO THAT.
TAKE IT FROM SOMEONE WHO KNOWS: YOU'LL NEED FRIENDS.
EXCEPT SUPER HEROES CALL THOSE FRIENDS "ALLIES."
I LIKE THE TERM "ALLIES" BETTER THAN "FRIENDS," ANYWAY.
SIGH
THIS CHAPTER'S ALL ABOUT ALLIES.

ONE THING!

THE GUARDIANS OF THE GALAXY SPEAK THE *TRUTH*. THE *MEASURE* OF A PERSON IS IN THE COMPANY HE OR SHE KEEPS. SUPER HEROES ARE ONLY AS GOOD AS THIER *FRIENDS*. FOR EXAMPLE, YOU COULD DO MUCH WORSE THAN TO HAVE A SABER-TOOTHED TIGER AS YOUR *NUMBER ONE* ALLY.* IN THIS CHAPTER, YOU WILL LEARN MUCH ABOUT ALLIES, AND YOU WILL MAKE A VERY IMPORTANT *ADDITION* TO YOUR MARVEL UNIVERSE SHEET:

ALLIES!

Yes, you will choose your Super Hero's closest friends, people who will drop what they are doing at a moment's notice to come to your aid.

*JUST ONE BIT OF FRIENDLY ADVICE: IF YOU USE A MEAT-SCENTED COLOGNE OR PERFUME, *STOP* WEARING IT. *IMMEDIATELY.*

You're going to encounter lots of Super Heroes on your adventures. Unlike relatives, but very much like your nose, you can pick your allies. Here are some helpful hints to guide you in the process.

TOP TEN

THINGS TO LOOK FOR IN AN ALLY

10. Should answer no to the question, "Are you a Super Villain?"

9. Knows where to buy purple pants in bulk

8. Has modestly appointed Adamantium-fortified battle fortress located on the moon

7. Can remember important dates, like your birthday

6. Doesn't hog dessert

5. Is quick to say, "I think we should call the Avengers"

4. Is an Avenger*

3. Is Hulk

2. Knows to take a bath every once in a while

1. Gets discount movie tickets

*AVENGERS MAKE **VERY** GOOD ALLIES.

TELL FRIEND FROM FOE!

YOU WILL MEET ALL KINDS OF PEOPLE IN THE SUPER HERO BUSINESS. SOME WILL BE *GOOD* GUYS, SOME WILL BE *BAD*. BUT *HOW* CAN YOU TELL THE DIFFERENCE? WE'VE PUT TOGETHER A THREE-POINT PLAN SO *SIMPLE*, A BABY COULD FOLLOW IT.*

POINT ONE: WHEN IN DOUBT, FIGHT IT OUT!

THIS ONE IS PRETTY MUCH A NO-BRAINER. THE FIRST TIME YOU MEET A POTENTIAL ALLY, YOU SHOULD FIGHT THEM. YOU DON'T REALLY NEED A REASON, BUT YOU'RE WELCOME TO INVENT ONE IF IT MAKES YOU FEEL BETTER.

SPURRED ON BY HIS BURNING HATRED FOR THE HUMAN RACE, THE RACE WHICH HAS HOUNDED AND TORMENTED HIM, THE RAMPAGING GREEN FIGURE ATTACKS WITHOUT WARNING!!

CAPTURE YOU?? BROTHER, I DON'T EVEN WANNA SHARE THE SAME *PLANET* WITH YOU!

EVEN HERE-- DEEP IN MY HIDDEN CAVES, YOU ATTACK ME! BUT *NO ONE* CAN CAPTURE THE *HULK!*

THE *IMPORTANT* THING IS, THE TWO OF YOU NEED TO PRETEND THAT YOU'RE REALLY SUPER VILLAINS AND FIGHT EACH OTHER ACCORDINGLY. WHEN YOU'RE DONE FIGHTING, YOU WILL HAVE A HEALTHY *RESPECT* FOR EACH OTHER'S ABILITIES, REALIZE THAT YOU'RE BOTH ON THE SIDE OF JUSTICE, AND BECOME *LIFELONG* FRIENDS.

*FIND US A BABY TO EXPLAIN IT TO US. WE CAN'T MAKE ANY SENSE OF IT.

POINT TWO: "NORTLU" SPELLED BACKWARD IS "ULTRON"

NORTLU

ULTRON

SAME GUY

BE ON THE LOOKOUT FOR SUPER VILLAINS WHO SPELL THEIR NAMES *BACKWARD*. THEY WILL USE THIS TO *CONFUSE* YOU INTO THINKING THEY ARE GOOD GUYS. IF YOU HAVE ALREADY FALLEN FOR THIS RUSE (AND IT IS A CLEVER ONE), *DON'T PANIC.** JUST ASK FOR A PIECE OF PAPER, THEN WRITE THE BACKWARD-SPELLED NAME FRONTWARD. IF IT'S THE NAME OF A BAD GUY YOU RECOGNIZE, THIS IS NOT AN ALLY.

*UNLESS THEY HAVE ALREADY CAPTURED YOU, IN WHICH CASE, REFER TO PAGE 94, STEP 3.

POINT THREE: VOCABULARY, VOCABULARY, VOCABULARY

PERHAPS THE BEST WAY OF TELLING *FRIEND* FROM *FOE* IS VOCABULARY. TAKE A LOOK AT THIS HANDY CHART, AND IF YOU HEAR ANY OF THESE STATEMENTS ESCAPE THE LIPS OF YOUR POTENTIAL ALLY, HEAD FOR THE HILLS.

THINGS A GOOD GUY DOESN'T SAY

I ROAM THE UNIVERSE IN SEARCH OF *REVENGE!*

THE *PENALTY* FOR FAILURE IS *DEATH!*

MY BUSINESS? *CONQUEST,* OF COURSE!

SERVE ME, OR *SUFFER* THE CONSEQUENCES!

FAREWELL, IRON MAN! ALL I NEED DO IS DROP MY DOLL FROM THIS HEIGHT AND YOU ARE *DOOMED!!*

MR. DOLL. SEE, THIS *ISN'T* SOMETHING A GOOD GUY SAYS.

You'll need all the **PRACTICE** you can get finding your super hero allies. We've created this incredibly **REALISTIC** simulation that looks **NOTHING LIKE A BOARD GAME** to help you do exactly that.

ALLIES, ASSEMBLE!

HOW TO PLAY!

1. Get your number dice. Use a penny for your Hero Token. Place it on **START**.

2. **Roll** the dice, and move that number of spaces. Follow the instructions on that space.

3. If you land on a **"GAIN AN ALLY!"** space, roll the dice and check the ally chart. **Choose** one of those heroes to be your ally, and write it in the space provided.

4. **Count** how many allies you have when you reach the finish.

5. **Congratulations!** You now have more allies than that Mr. Doll guy.

PICK YOUR ALLY!

WHO ARE YOUR ALLIES?

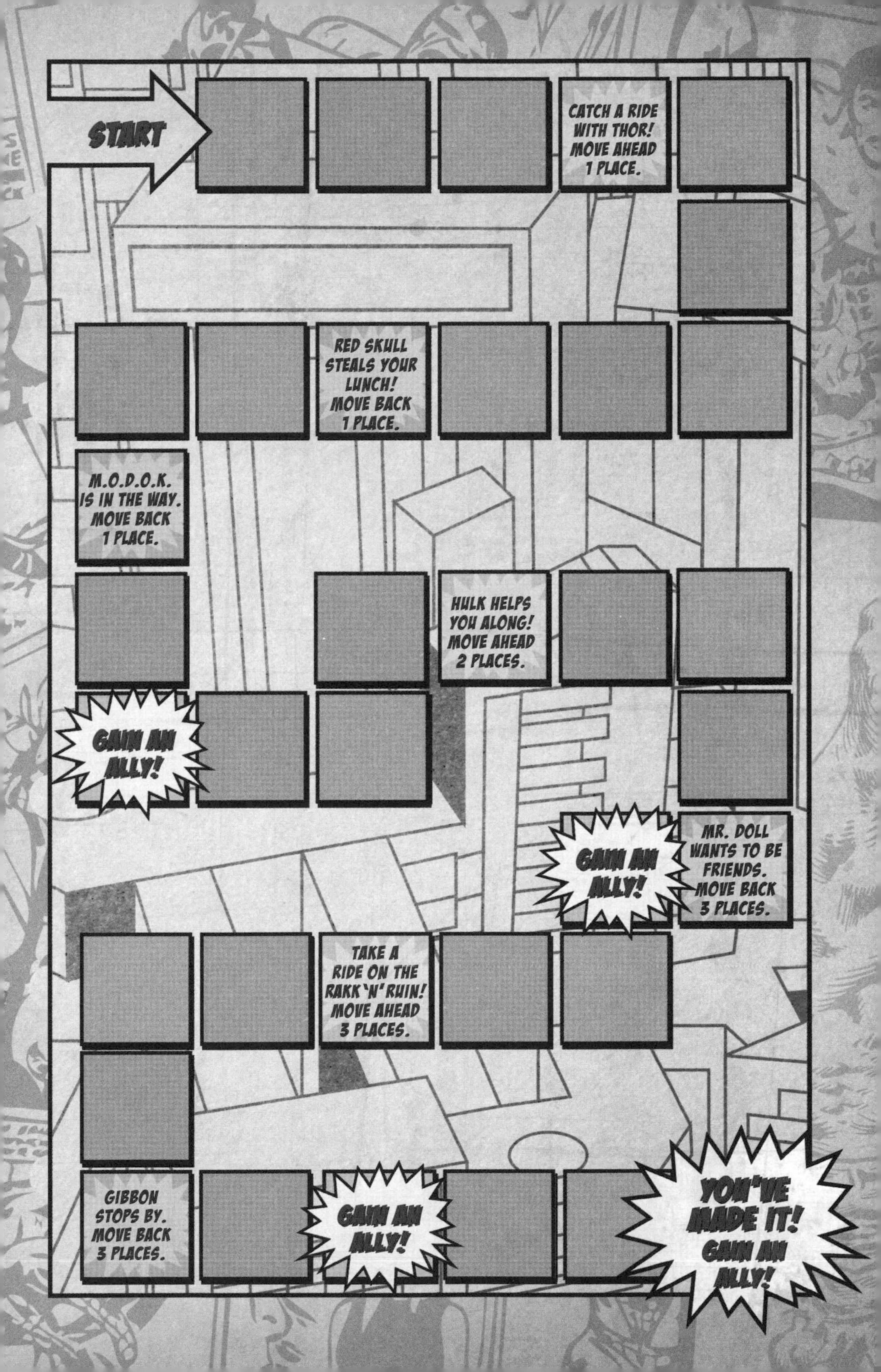
START
CATCH A RIDE WITH THOR! MOVE AHEAD 1 PLACE.
RED SKULL STEALS YOUR LUNCH! MOVE BACK 1 PLACE.
M.O.D.O.K. IS IN THE WAY. MOVE BACK 1 PLACE.
HULK HELPS YOU ALONG! MOVE AHEAD 2 PLACES.
GAIN AN ALLY!
GAIN AN ALLY!
MR. DOLL WANTS TO BE FRIENDS. MOVE BACK 3 PLACES.
TAKE A RIDE ON THE RAKK 'N' RUIN! MOVE AHEAD 3 PLACES.
GIBBON STOPS BY. MOVE BACK 3 PLACES.
GAIN AN ALLY!
YOU'VE MADE IT! GAIN AN ALLY!

THERE HAVE BEEN SOME ASTONISHING HERO *TEAM-UPS* THROUGHOUT THE HISTORY OF SUPER HERODOM. CAPTAIN AMERICA AND FALCON. ANT-MAN AND WASP. SPIDER-MAN AND WHOMEVER HE TEAMED UP WITH. IN OUR *NEVER-ENDING** QUEST TO IMPART ALL WE KNOW ABOUT ALLIES, READ ON TO DISCOVER SOME *AMAZING* AND *LESS-THAN-AMAZING* PARTNERSHIPS.

GREAT (AND NOT-SO-GREAT) TEAM-UPS

CAPTAIN AMERICA AND FALCON

WHAT MAKES THEM GREAT: These two heroes mesh so well, it's hard to tell where one ends and the other begins. Both are idealistic and driven to the cause of justice.

ANT-MAN AND WASP

WHAT MAKES THEM GREAT: Science-based heroes don't come any smaller (or smarter) than these two. Their size-changing powers confuse bad guys like no one's business.

*IT ENDS ON PAGE *122.*

MOON GIRL AND DEVIL DINOSAUR

WHAT MAKES THEM GREAT: Are you kidding? Team a super-smart girl with a fearsome *T. rex* and you have the recipe for a pair of allies who can kick some bad-guy butt.

CAPTAIN AMERICA AND A BROCCOLI-HEADED ALIEN

WHAT MAKES THEM NOT-SO-GREAT: The broccoli-headed alien started out as kind of a bad guy, but then he wasn't so bad, and Captain America helped him, sort of. It's complicated.

ANT-MAN AND AN ARROW

WHAT MAKES THEM NOT-SO-GREAT: The arrow couldn't speak, it was really terrible at strategy, and at the end of the day, Ant-Man had to team up with Hawkeye instead.

IT'S AMAZING THE DIFFERENCE ONE LETTER CAN MAKE. WHY, JUST LETTING AN *"ALLY"* NEAR THE LETTER *E* WILL TURN IT INTO AN *"ALLEY"!* IN THE INTEREST OF MAKING THIS WHOLE *"GET AN ALLY"* THING FOOLPROOF, WE'VE TEASED OUT THE DIFFERENCES BETWEEN AN ALLY AND AN ALLEY.

ALLY VS. ALLEY!

ALLY

A PERSON ASSOCIATED WITH A COMMON CAUSE

KEEPS YOUR SECRETS

HELPS DEFEAT BAD GUYS

IS ALWAYS THERE FOR YOU

CLEANS UP HUMAN GARBAGE

ALLEY

A NARROW BACK STREET OR PASSAGE

KEEPS YOUR TRASH

HELPS YOU GET FROM ONE STREET TO ANOTHER

IS ALWAYS THERE (ALLEYS CAN'T MOVE)

FULL OF HUMANS' GARBAGE

110

WHAT DO YOU DO WHEN YOU NEED AN ALLY BUT EVERYONE'S BUSY? HERE ARE THE TOP CHOICES OF THE SUPER HEROES WHEN HELP IS IN SHORT SUPPLY.

CHIMPS AHOY!

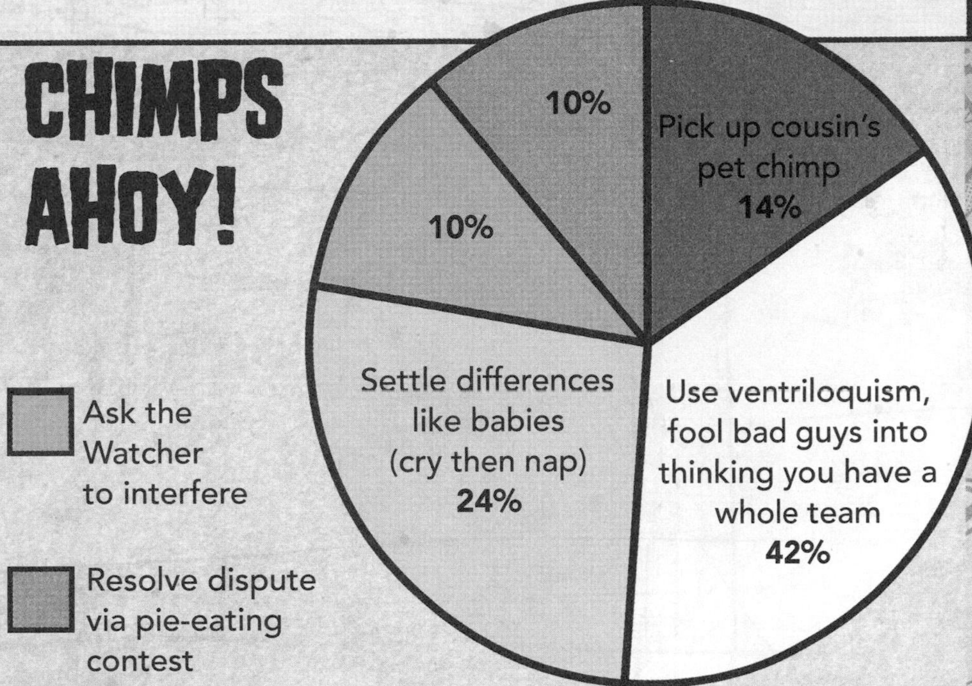
10%
Pick up cousin's pet chimp 14%
10%
Settle differences like babies (cry then nap) 24%
Use ventriloquism, fool bad guys into thinking you have a whole team 42%
Ask the Watcher to interfere
Resolve dispute via pie-eating contest

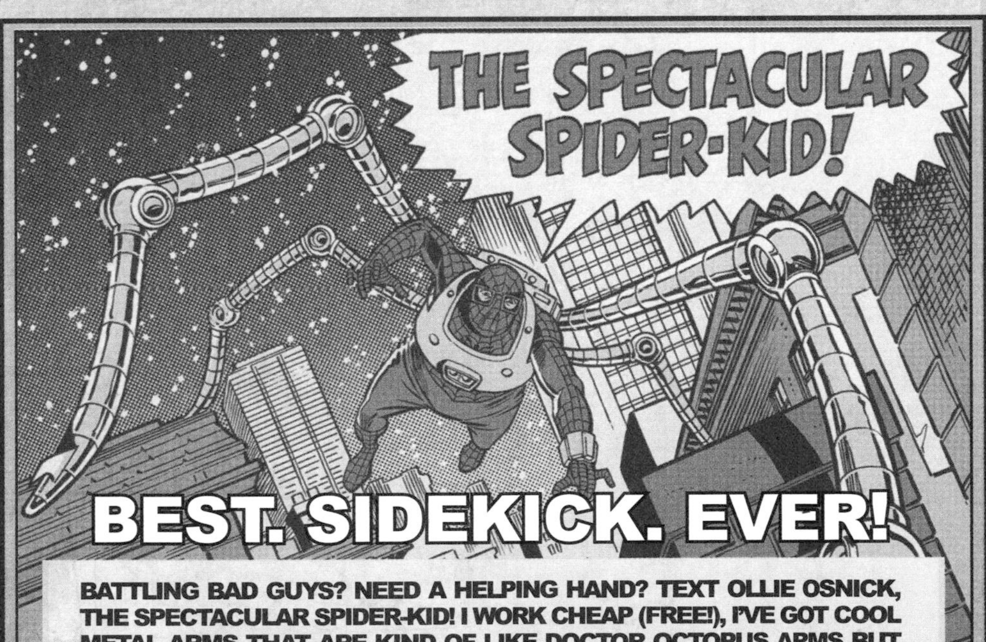
THE SPECTACULAR SPIDER-KID!
BEST. SIDEKICK. EVER!
BATTLING BAD GUYS? NEED A HELPING HAND? TEXT OLLIE OSNICK, THE SPECTACULAR SPIDER-KID! I WORK CHEAP (FREE!), I'VE GOT COOL METAL ARMS THAT ARE KIND OF LIKE DOCTOR OCTOPUS ARMS BUT ALSO KIND OF LIKE SPIDER ARMS, AND I DON'T ASK ANY QUESTIONS!

WE ASKED DOCTOR STRANGE TO COME UP WITH SOMETHING FOR WHEN YOU NEED AN ALLY AND YOU NEED *ONE RIGHT AWAY.* *HERE'S* WHAT THE DOCTOR ORDERED!

INSTANT ALLY

THE SETUP
1. *STARE* AT THE PICTURE BELOW FOR APPROXIMATELY ONE MINUTE, FOCUSING ON THE WHITE DOT.
2. *NO* BLINKING.
3. NOW *STARE* AT A BLANK (WHITE) WALL AND BLINK. YOU WILL SEE THE IMAGE OF YOUR ALLY!

YOU'D THINK MORE WORDS WOULD RHYME WITH "*ALLY.*"
CLOSE . . . *SO CLOSE.*

WORDS THAT ALMOST RHYME
WITH "ALLY"

10. Alloy

9. Badly

8. Galley

7. Happy

6. Valley

5. Carry

4. Alice

3. Rally

2. Snappy

1. Crabby

BY THE DEMONS OF DARKNESS,

IN THE NAME OF SATANNISH,

BY THE FLAMES OF THE FALTINE,

LET THE PERSON WHO WROTE THIS . . .

VANISH!

THE MORE WE THOUGHT ABOUT IT, THE MORE IT MADE SENSE TO JUST *GIVE* YOU A WHOLE BUNCH OF *ALLIES* THAT YOU COULD CUT OUT AND MAKE! THIS WAY, YOU'LL *ALWAYS* HAVE PLENTY OF HEROES ON HAND TO GO UP AGAINST THE LIKES OF THE *GIBBON.**

ALLIED ARMY!

WHAT YOU'LL NEED

- A piece of cardboard
- A glue stick
- Scissors
- An adult human-type being with access to a color copier

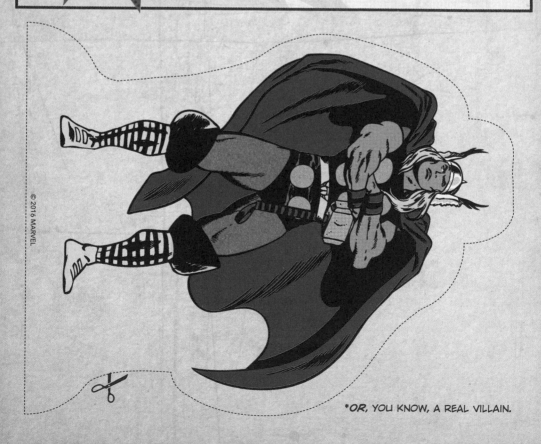

*OR, YOU KNOW, A REAL VILLAIN.

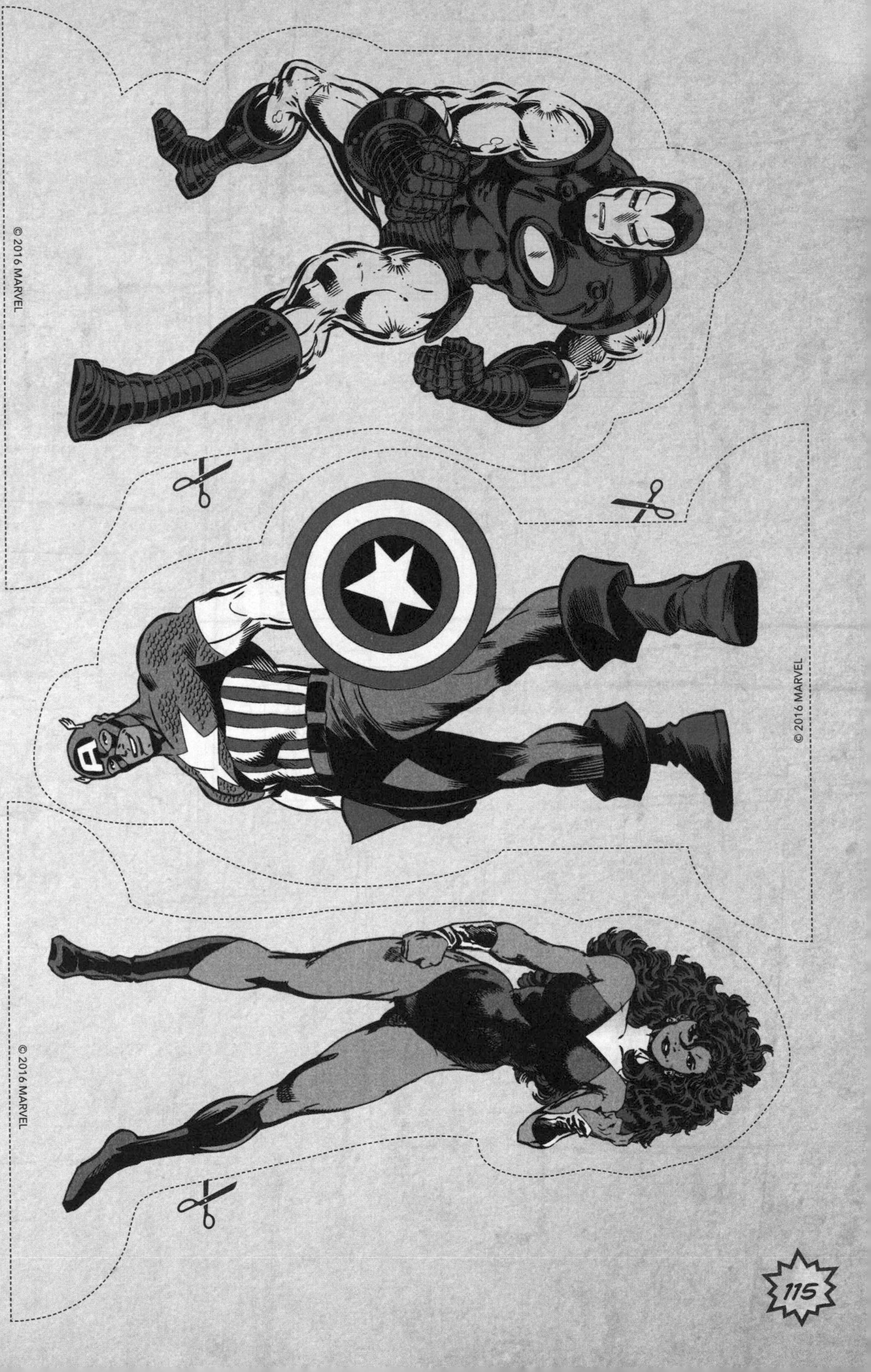

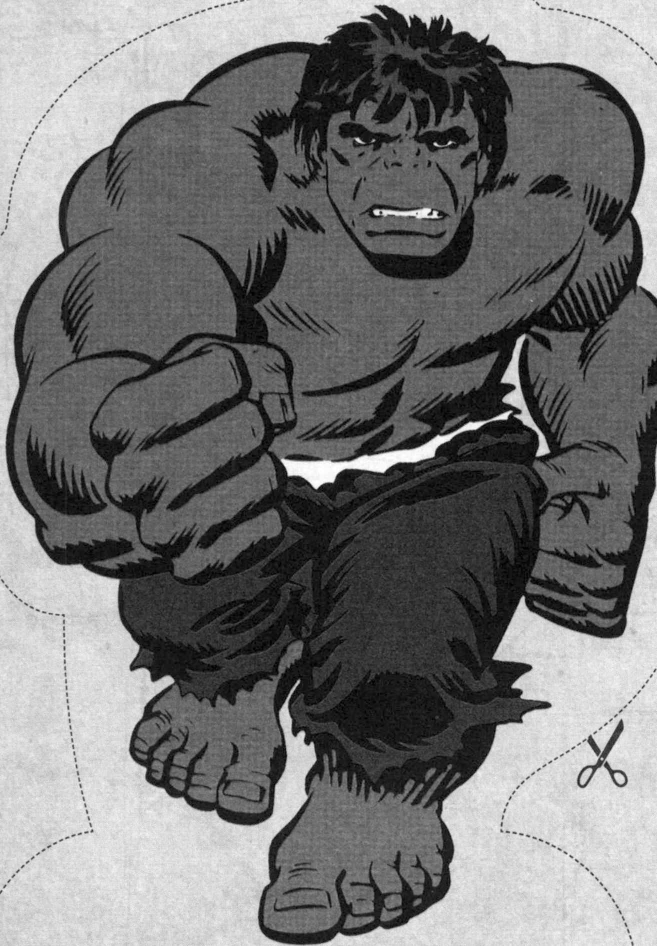

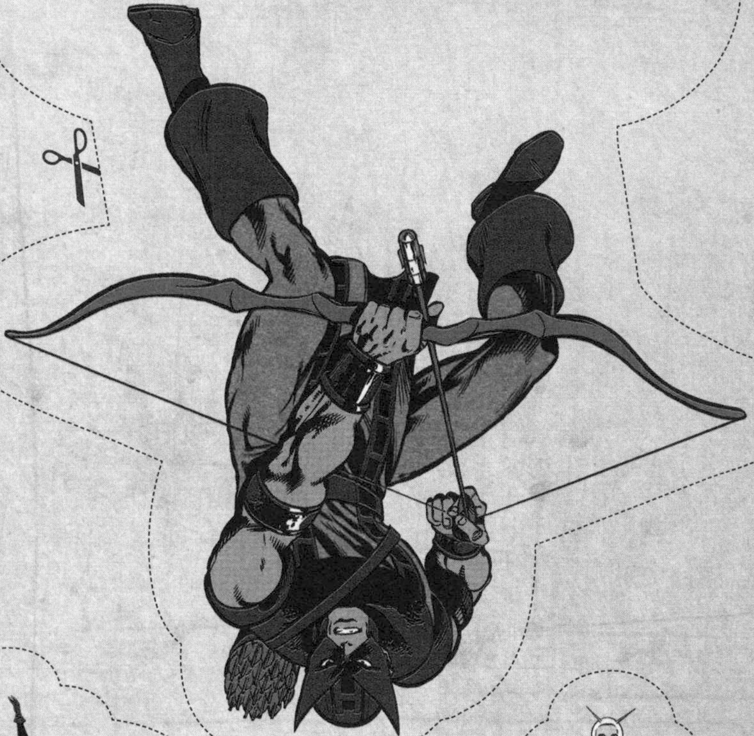

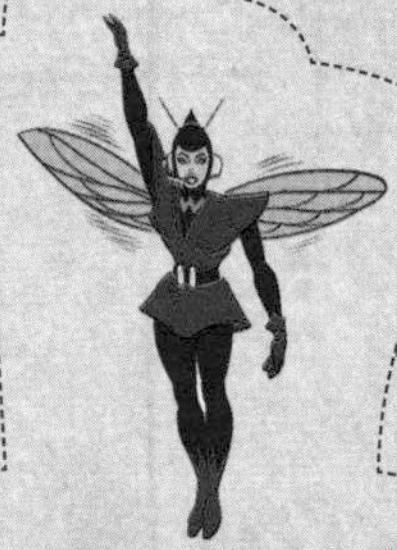

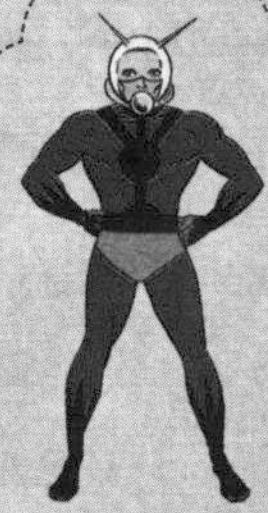

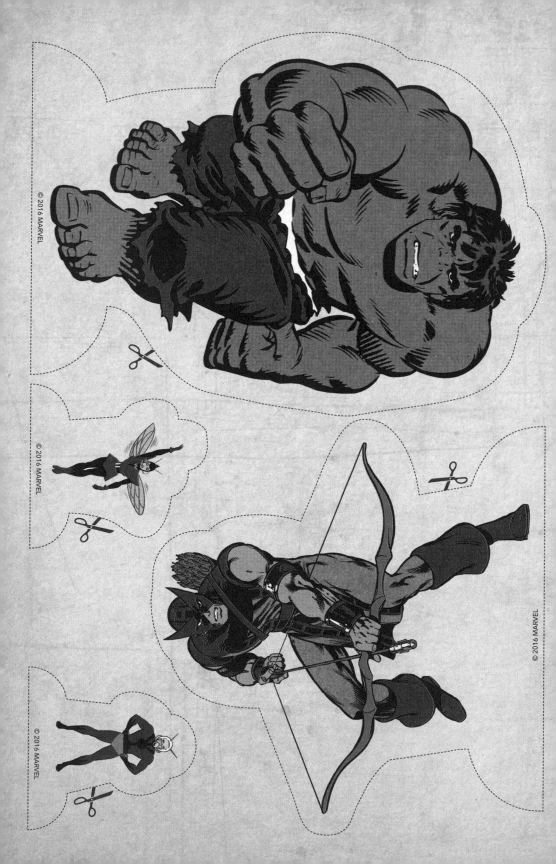

THE SETUP

ASK AN ADULT TO MAKE COLOR COPIES OF THE ALLY PAGES.

WITH NOTHING BUT YOUR GLUE STICK AND A DREAM, **STICK** THE COLOR COPIES TO THE CARDBOARD. **LET** DRY.

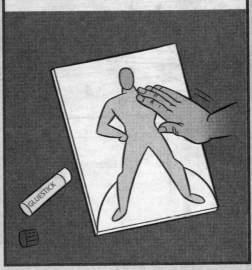

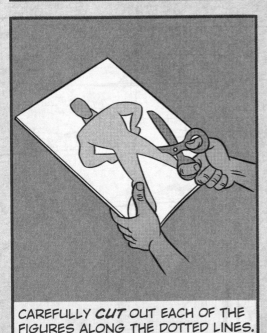

CAREFULLY **CUT** OUT EACH OF THE FIGURES ALONG THE DOTTED LINES.

FOLD THE TWO TABS AT THE BASE OF EACH FIGURE TO MAKE THEM STAND UP.

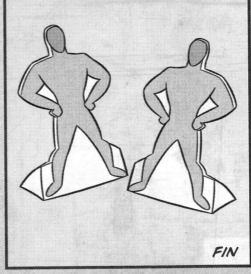

FIN

NOW SCOOP UP YOUR ARMY OF ALLIES AND TAKE THEM WITH YOU WHEREVER YOU GO!

SOME PEOPLE THINK THAT VARIETY IS THE SPICE OF LIFE. BUT IT'S NOT. YOU KNOW WHAT IS? *FILLING* OUT FORMS AND SUBMITTING THEM TO *S.H.I.E.L.D.*! AND THAT'S JUST WHAT YOU'RE GOING TO DO. *FILL* OUT THIS FORM AND *SUBMIT* IT TO *S.H.I.E.L.D.* WITH YOUR *RA-1* REQUEST!*

FORM RA-1!

WHAT YOU NEED TO DO: *FILL* OUT THE ANSWERS TO THE QUESTIONS ON THIS FORM. WHEN YOU'RE DONE, *SEND* A COPY TO THIS ADDRESS:

MARVEL'S AGENTS OF *S.H.I.E.L.D.*

YOU'LL BE *NOTIFIED* IF YOUR REQUEST HAS BEEN ACCEPTED.

*RA-1 REQUEST = *REQUEST ASSISTANCE REQUEST*. WE KNOW THAT'S *REDUNDANT*, BUT THAT'S BUREAUCRACY FOR YOU.

Form RA-1

S.H.I.E.L.D. FORM RA-1 (October 20____)

Official Request Assistance Request to Director Fury

From: _____ *(Your name)*

Date: _____

Super Hero Name: _____

Reason for Form RA-1 Request: _____
_____
_____
_____

Please Note Names of Any Super Heroes Requested *(you may enter up to 8 names but no fewer than 5, unless request is made on an odd-numbered Friday, when you may request 9 names):*
_____   _____   _____
_____   _____   _____
_____   _____   _____

Hazards You Expect to Encounter: _____
_____
_____
_____
_____
_____

# of Days Assistance Will Be Required: _____

Will Mission Occur Off-Planet? Y / N *(Circle one but not both, unless the answer is "maybe")*

If Answer Was "Yes," Please List Name of Planet: _____

At Any Time in the Mission Do You Expect to Call Director Fury in a Panic? Y / N *(Circle one)*

If "Yes," explain using S.H.I.E.L.D. Code Priority Ultra: _____
_____

If You Have No Idea What S.H.I.E.L.D. Code Priority Ultra Is, Please Use Form RA-2 *(file separately).*

Favorite Breakfast Food: _____

Signature _____

Print Name _____

Date _____

WE KNEW THIS TIME
WOULD COME—THE TIME
WHEN YOU WILL SELECT
YOUR *ALLIES* TO WRITE ON
YOUR MARVEL UNIVERSE SHEET!
FOLLOW THE INSTRUCTIONS
BELOW, THEN ENTER THE INFORMATION
ON PAGE 166.

KNOWN ALLIES!

HERE'S WHAT YOU DO:
TAKE THE *ATTRIBUTE* AND
NUMBER DICE. *ROLL* THE
DICE, MAKING NOTE OF THE
ICON AND NUMBER THAT
COME UP. *FIND* THEM IN THE
CHART ON PAGE 121. YOU
CAN *PICK ONE ALLY* FOR
EACH ICON AND NUMBER
THAT YOU ROLLED. IF YOU
ROLLED A 6, YOU CAN PICK
ONE MORE ALLY FROM
ANYWHERE ON THE PAGE!
DON'T SEE A SUPER
HERO ALLY YOU LIKE?

YOU CAN ALSO
WRITE IN YOUR *OWN*
ALLIES USING THE
BLANK SPACES!

① ATTRIBUTES!

1. INTELLIGENCE

DOCTOR STRANGE
IRON MAN

2. STRENGTH

HULK
CAPTAIN MARVEL

3. SPEED

QUICKSILVER
NOVA

4. DURABILITY

WHITE TIGER
WAR MACHINE

5. ENERGY PROJECTION

THOR
SPIDER-WOMAN

6. FIGHTING

BLACK WIDOW
FALCON

② SPECIAL POWERS!

SPIDER-MAN
SPIDER-HAM

AGENT PHIL COULSON
J. JONAH JAMESON
(SORRY, WE DON'T
MAKE THE RULES.)

GROOT
ROCKET RACCOON

GAMORA
STAR-LORD

SQUIRREL GIRL
SPEEDBALL

WEREWOLF BY NIGHT
FRANKENSTEIN'S
MONSTER

YOU KNOW WHAT'S IRONIC? IN A CHAPTER ALL ABOUT *ALLIES* AND *TEAMWORK* AND *ASKING* FOR HELP, YOU HAVE TO TAKE THIS QUIZ ALL BY YOURSELF WITH HELP FROM NOBODY. ISN'T THAT *FUNNY?*

LITTLE HELP HERE?

1 Spider-Kid's real name is:

OLLIE OLLIE OXEN FREE **OR** OLLIE OSNICK

2 Which of the following is **NOT** something to look for in an ally?

SOMEONE WHO DOESN'T HOG DESSERT **OR** SOMEONE WHO DOES DESSERT HOGS

3 Is it us, or did that last question make, like, **ZERO** sense?

IT MADE, LIKE, ZERO SENSE **OR** BASICALLY UNDERSTOOD IT, KIND OF

4 If you meet someone named Nortlu, you will:

CALL S.H.I.E.L.D. FOR BACKUP **OR** HELP HIM TAKE OVER THE WORLD (HE SEEMS NICE)

5 Mr. Doll? Really?

REALLY **OR** WHERE DID YOU DIG HIM UP?

YOU CAN REARRANGE THE LETTERS IN "*ENEMIES*" TO SPELL "*I SEEN ME!*"

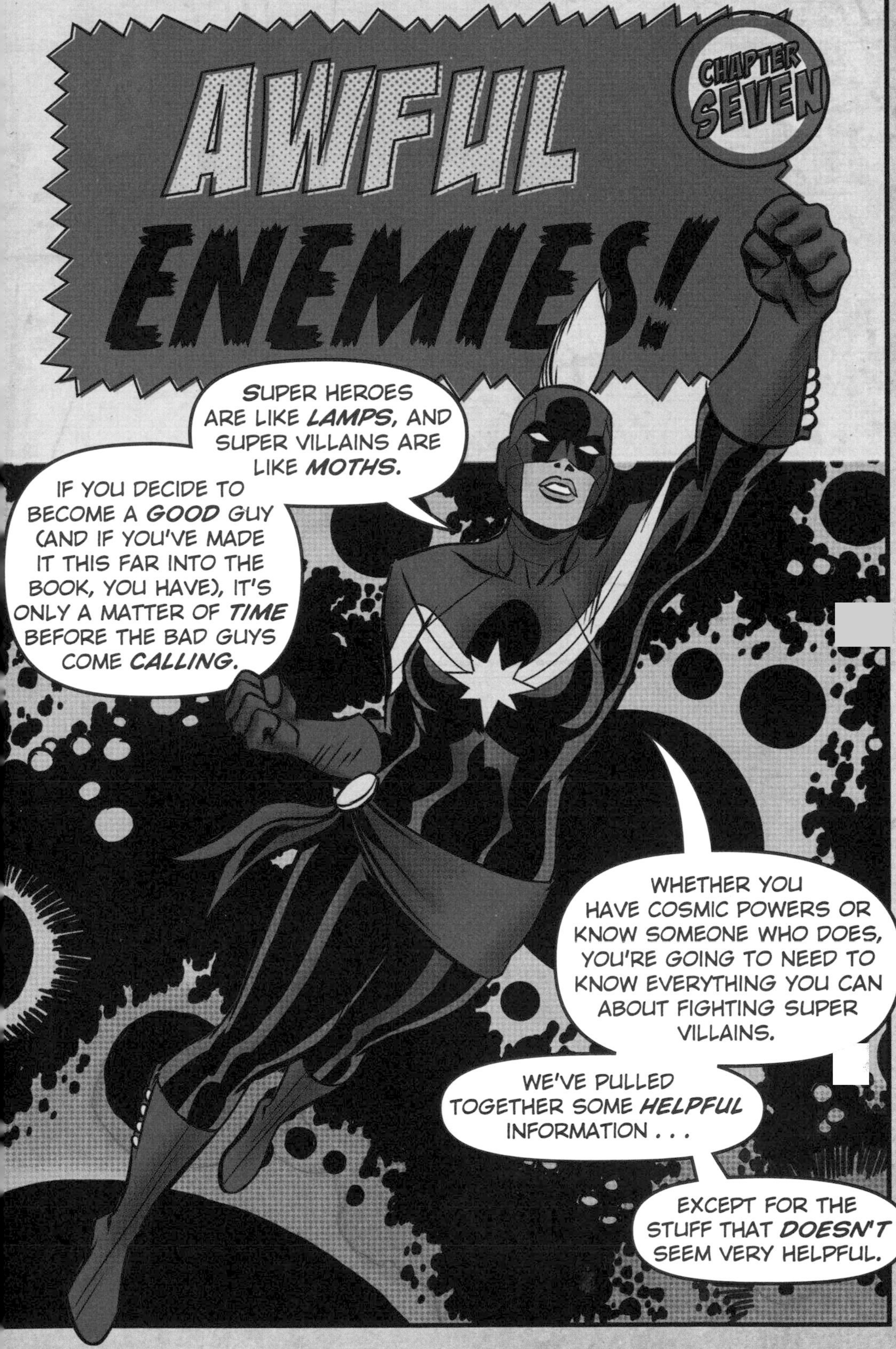
CHAPTER SEVEN
AWFUL ENEMIES!
SUPER HEROES ARE LIKE *LAMPS,* AND SUPER VILLAINS ARE LIKE *MOTHS.*
IF YOU DECIDE TO BECOME A *GOOD* GUY (AND IF YOU'VE MADE IT THIS FAR INTO THE BOOK, YOU HAVE), IT'S ONLY A MATTER OF *TIME* BEFORE THE BAD GUYS COME *CALLING.*
WHETHER YOU HAVE COSMIC POWERS OR KNOW SOMEONE WHO DOES, YOU'RE GOING TO NEED TO KNOW EVERYTHING YOU CAN ABOUT FIGHTING SUPER VILLAINS.
WE'VE PULLED TOGETHER SOME *HELPFUL* INFORMATION . . .
EXCEPT FOR THE STUFF THAT *DOESN'T* SEEM VERY HELPFUL.

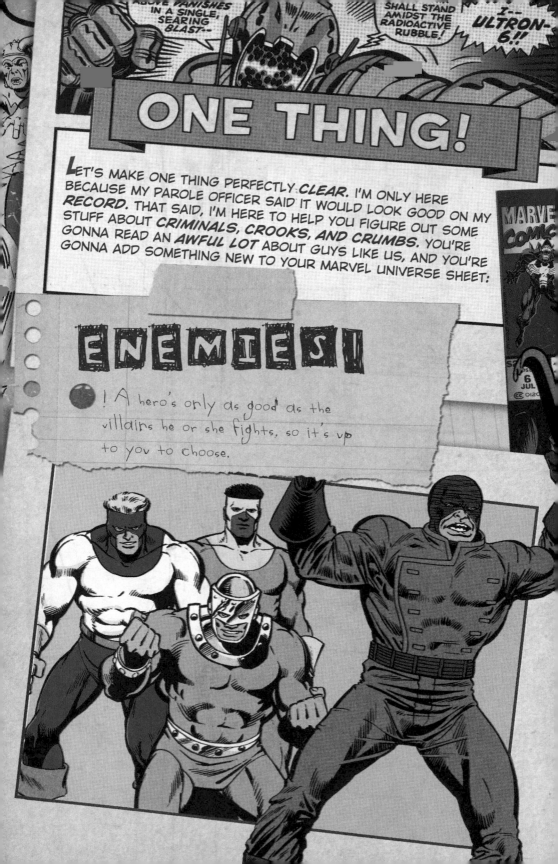

ONE THING!

LET'S MAKE ONE THING PERFECTLY *CLEAR*. I'M ONLY HERE BECAUSE MY PAROLE OFFICER SAID IT WOULD LOOK GOOD ON MY *RECORD*. THAT SAID, I'M HERE TO HELP YOU FIGURE OUT SOME STUFF ABOUT *CRIMINALS, CROOKS, AND CRUMBS*. YOU'RE GONNA READ AN *AWFUL LOT* ABOUT GUYS LIKE US, AND YOU'RE GONNA ADD SOMETHING NEW TO YOUR MARVEL UNIVERSE SHEET:

ENEMIES!

● ! A hero's only as good as the villains he or she fights, so it's up to you to choose.

Sometimes the bad guys make plans that seem so *SINISTER*, you'd think they were like *HOMEWORK* . . . or *WORSE*. Read on to discover some of the best (worst?) of each.

MOST EVIL
SUPER VILLAIN SCHEMES
OR HOMEWORK ASSIGNMENTS

10. Blow up moon

9. Read thirty chapters in one night (good luck with that)

8. Decide humanity's the problem, use robot army to take over Earth

7. Carry grudge from World War II to present day, attack Captain America

6. Make authentic pioneer cabin with macaroni and glue

5. Follow Spider-Man home, discover secret identity

4. Prepare for test using nothing but a toothpick and goose fat

3. Find Infinity Gems, take over known universe

2. Create Life Model Decoys of world leaders

1. Tie: assemble all-new Masters of Evil team / math

SURELY, ASSEMBLING THE *INFINITY GEMS* AND TAKING OVER THE UNIVERSE IS MORE *SINISTER* THAN MATH?

KNOW YOUR BAD GUYS!

IF YOU'RE GOING OUT INTO THE FIELD, YOU'RE GOING TO *NEED* TO KNOW WHO'S WHO. HERE'S A *BRIEF* RUNDOWN OF SOME OF THE *SUPER VILLAINS* YOU'RE *LIKELY* TO ENCOUNTER.

DOCTOR OCTOPUS

HIS DEAL: Deranged scientist sporting four metal arms that obey his every whim

HATES: Spider-Man

DORMAMMU

HIS DEAL: Flame-headed magic guy who rules the Dark Dimension

HATES: Doctor Strange

M.O.D.O.K.

HIS DEAL: Former janitor, now big-headed brain guy in a floating chair

HATES: Iron Man, the Avengers

BARON ZEMO

HIS DEAL: Deranged scientist whose mask is glued to his face

HATES: Captain America, the Avengers, having a mask glued to his face

LOKI

HIS DEAL: Norse god of evil, but that seems so subjective

HATES: Accursed brother, Thor

RED SKULL

HIS DEAL: Skull-faced bad guy created during World War II

HATES: Captain America

GREEN GOBLIN

HIS DEAL: Evil businessman turned evil Super Villain; hard to explain the goblin suit

HATES: Spider-Man

TASKMASTER

HIS DEAL: Bad guy with "photographic reflexes"(can copy any moves)

HATES: Most Super Heroes, long walks on sandy beaches

KANGAROO

HIS DEAL: Former boxer who hung out with kangaroos, got kangaroo powers (sort of)

HATES: Anyone who points out that having kangaroo powers is not impressive

MAYBE THEY DIDN'T GET HUGGED ENOUGH AS CHILDREN. *MAYBE* NO ONE EVER LISTENED TO THEM FOR HOURS ON END AS THEY BLABBED ENDLESSLY ABOUT THIS OR THAT. ONE THING'S FOR SURE, SUPER VILLAINS *LOVE* TO TALK. *A LOT.* IF YOU CAN GET SUPER VILLAINS TALKING, ODDS ARE GOOD THAT THEY WILL EVENTUALLY TELL YOU EVERYTHING ABOUT THEIR *PLANS.* HERE ARE SOME HANDY TIPS TO GUIDE YOU.

MAKE A BAD GUY TALK A LOT AND REVEAL THE EVIL SCHEME

HOW YOU DO IT!

1. **Allow** yourself to be captured. If you are not a very good Super Hero, this will look more like you're just getting captured, period.

2. **Ask** lots of questions. Bad guys **like** this. Make sure the questions are about the bad guy, though. Don't ask about sports scores or recipes.

3. Once the talk is flowing, try casually slipping in this question: "**What** is your plan?"

4. The bad guy will **tell** you the plan.

5. **Call** the Avengers.

128

asked, Dr. Connors could not initially explain why the

Thing" instead of "Thing-Man." "I think it's alphabetical, maybe?"

Th
Ma
ma

DEAR THOR
Oh, Brother . . .

BY THOR, SON OF ODIN THE ONE-EYED, WIELDER OF MJOLNIR, GOD OF THUNDER

DEAR THOR: I have a problem, and I'm wondering if you could take a break from acting so special to help me. My brother, we'll call him Thorp, is the biggest pain. I'm not kidding, he's the biggest. Everyone loves him and even Mom and Dad think he's sooooo cool and worthy of holding a magic hammer. Not that he has a magic hammer! I mean, they just think he's worthy. I'm sure you can relate. Anyway, all I want to do is cast a spell and summon a bunch of trolls to take him away to work in their underground mines forever. Cool/not cool?

SIGNED, UH, BILL

DEAR UH, BILL: Verily, 'tis a problem most perplexing. On hand the one, this Thorp is thy brother. He is kin, and thou shouldst love one another. On hand the other, truly he sounds like a jerk, as mine Midgard comrades would say. Though eternal banishment to the lair of trolls doth seem extreme, thou must do as thou see fit.

SIGNED, THOR

Everyone has a problem. What is yours? For a personal reply, write to Thor, son of Odin the one-eyed, wielder of Mjolnir, god of thunder, 1 Bifrost Bridge, Valhalla, and enclose a stamped, self-addressed envelope.

Don't miss out on any of Thor's otherworldly advice. Subscribe to THE DAILY BUGLE TODAY!

C
C
M
th
ac

W

Tha
call
York
up S
liqui
wrec
Contr
look
little

I Like Socks!

VE ALL NEED MORE GOLD-
OE SOCKS IN OUR LIVES.
HEY'RE COMFORTABLE,
FFORDABLE A

Why would anyone want to wear anything BUT gold-toe socks? You wouldn't

It's been said that heroes and villains are just two sides of the same coin. We're not sure if there's any truth to that or not. But we ARE sure that you'll need a coin to play this game.

TWO SIDES OF THE SAME COIN!

WHAT YOU'LL NEED

- A two-sided coin
- A friend or enemy to play with
- If you don't want to mark up the book, ask an adult to make a color copy of this game

HOW TO PLAY!

1. If only we had some way of determining who goes first. Like, something we could flip . . .

2. **Take** turns flipping the coin. **Heads = good guy, tails = bad guy**. If the coin lands on heads, cross out a good guy space on your card. If the coin lands on tails, cross out a bad guy space.

3. Whoever crosses out all the bad guy spaces on their card first wins.

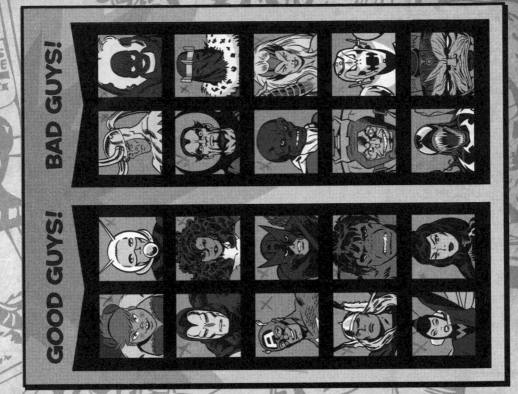

BAD GUYS!

GOOD GUYS!

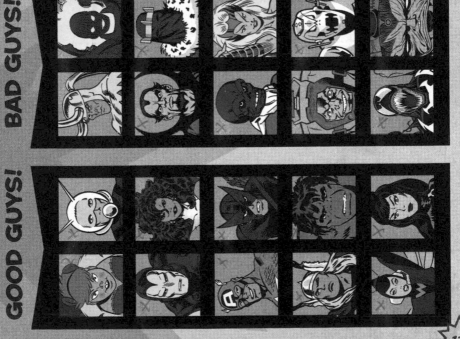

BAD GUYS!

GOOD GUYS!

131

WHY DO VILLAINS DO IT? ***WHY*** ARE THEY ***SO*** BAD? WE ASKED A ***RANDOM*** GROUP OF SUPER VILLAINS. ***HERE*** ARE THEIR TOP ANSWERS!

WHY?

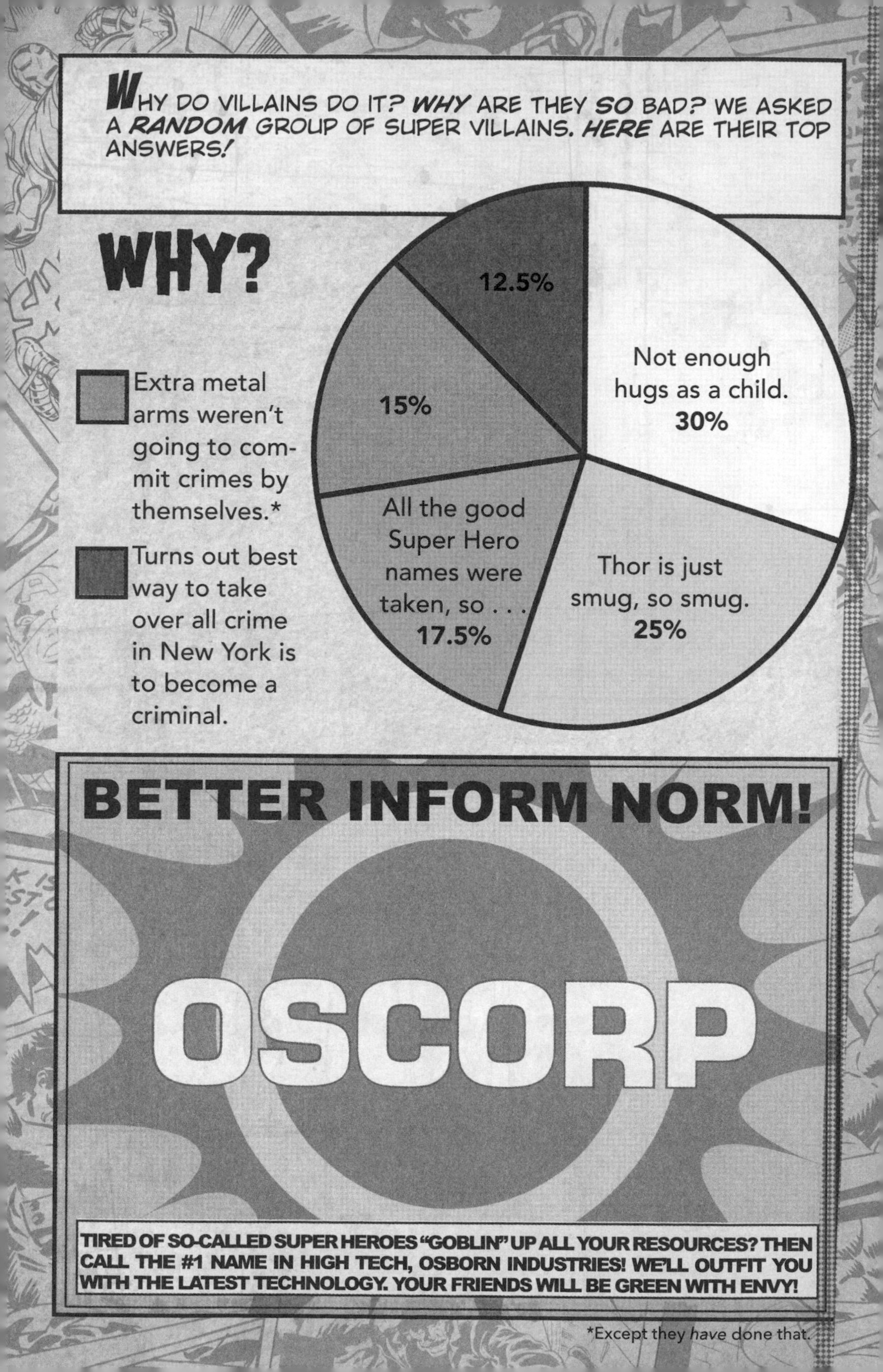

12.5%
Not enough hugs as a child.
30%
15%
All the good Super Hero names were taken, so . . .
17.5%
Thor is just smug, so smug.
25%

- Extra metal arms weren't going to commit crimes by themselves.*
- Turns out best way to take over all crime in New York is to become a criminal.

BETTER INFORM NORM!

OSCORP

TIRED OF SO-CALLED SUPER HEROES "GOBLIN" UP ALL YOUR RESOURCES? THEN CALL THE #1 NAME IN HIGH TECH, OSBORN INDUSTRIES! WE'LL OUTFIT YOU WITH THE LATEST TECHNOLOGY. YOUR FRIENDS WILL BE GREEN WITH ENVY!

*Except they *have* done that.

*I*T WAS BOUND TO HAPPEN. BAD GUYS GET TIRED OF HAVING THEIR MASKS HANDED TO THEM, SO THEY DECIDE TO SWITCH SIDES. *GOOD ON THEM!* IN CASE YOU ENCOUNTER THEM IN THE FIELD, HERE ARE JUST A FEW OF THE FORMER SUPER VILLAINS WHO ARE NOW SUPER HEROES. IN OTHER WORDS, *DO NOT* HIT THEM.

WHEN BAD GUYS GO GOOD

BLACK WIDOW

Once a spy intent on stealing secrets from Tony Stark, Black Widow switched sides to become a hero.

HAWKEYE

He didn't mean to be a bad guy, but everyone thought he was. Then he meant to be a good guy, and everyone thought he wasn't, until they did.

BLACK CAT

This burglar used to bedevil Spider-Man, and then she reformed kind of. Mostly.

PROWLER

This burglar used to bedevil Spider-Man, and then he reformed. Totally reformed.

SPIDER-WOMAN

She used to work for Hydra, which was a bummer. She eventually became an Avenger.

WONDER MAN

Created by Baron Zemo to destroy the Avengers, Wonder Man did the exact opposite and joined the team. Better luck next time, Baron.

I**N THE PREVIOUS CHAPTER, YOU MADE A WHOLE *BUNCH* OF SUPER HEROES TO ASSEMBLE YOUR OWN *MIGHTY* TEAM. THEY WOULDN'T BE HEROES IF THEY DIDN'T HAVE A *BUNCH* OF SUPER VILLAINS TO OPPOSE, WOULD THEY? *NO*, NO THEY WOULDN'T. SO GET READY TO *GLUE! CUT! FOLD! PLAY!* IN THAT ORDER!**

BRING ON THE BAD GUYS!

WHAT YOU'LL NEED

- A piece of cardboard
- A glue stick
- Scissors
- An adult human-type being with access to a color copier

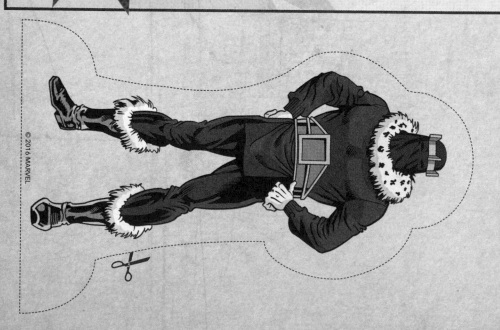

© 2016 MARVEL

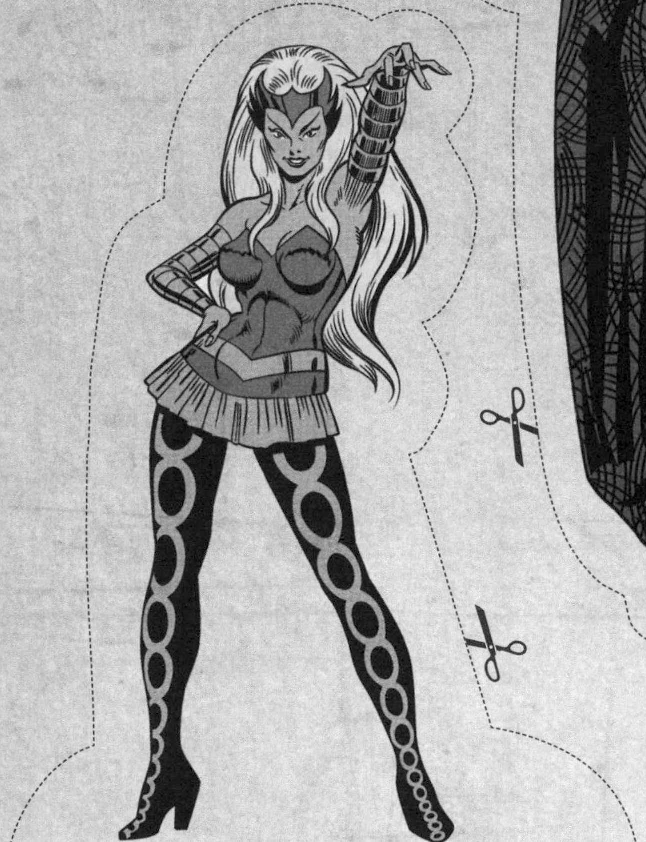

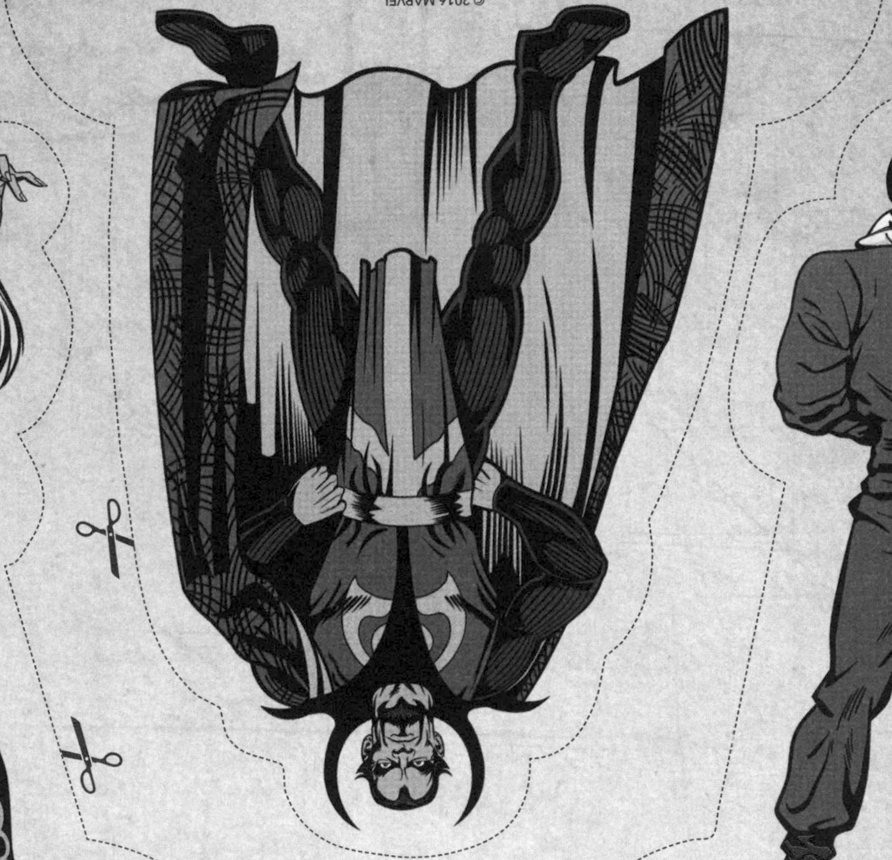

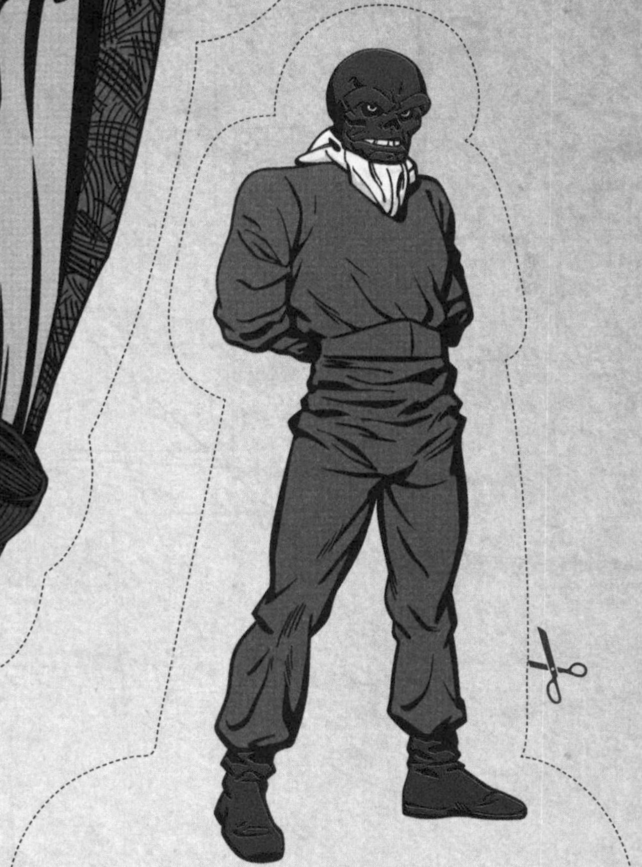

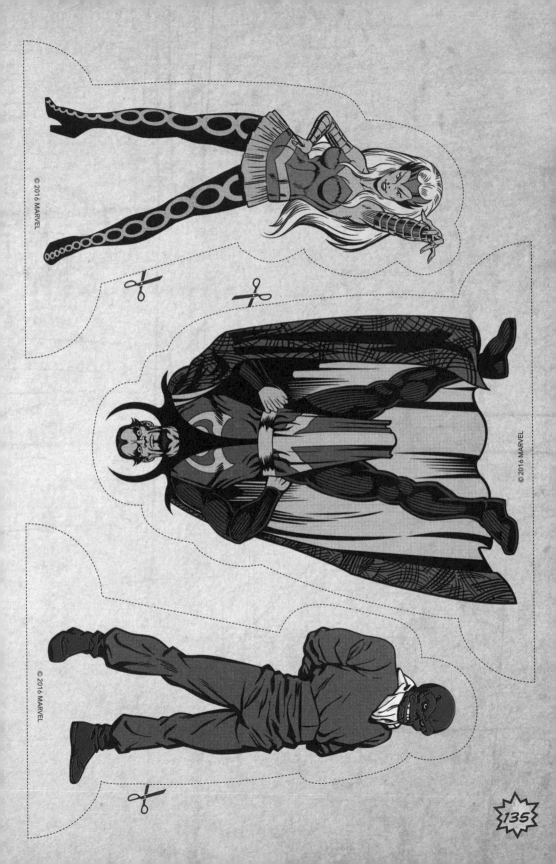

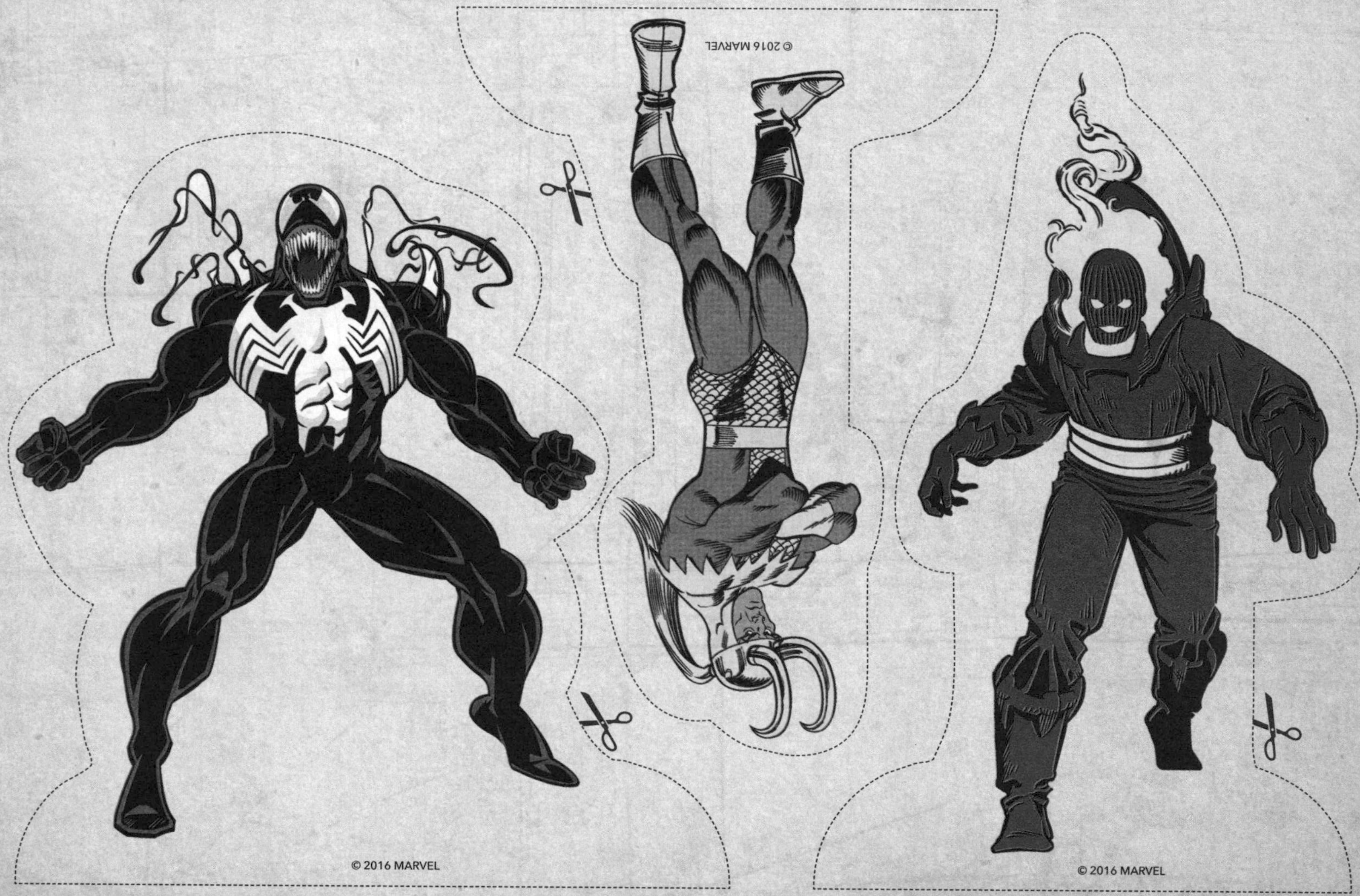
© 2016 MARVEL
© 2016 MARVEL
© 2016 MARVEL

THE SETUP

ASK AN ADULT TO MAKE COLOR COPIES OF THE VILLAIN PAGES.

WITH NOTHING BUT YOUR GLUE STICK AND A DREAM, *STICK* THE COLOR COPIES TO THE CARDBOARD. *LET* DRY.

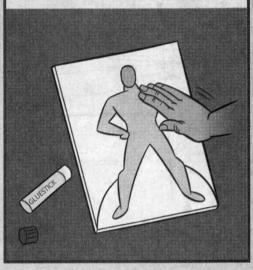

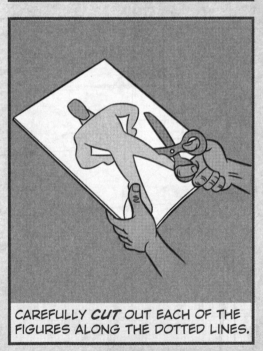

CAREFULLY *CUT* OUT EACH OF THE FIGURES ALONG THE DOTTED LINES.

FOLD THE TWO TABS AT THE BASE OF EACH FIGURE TO MAKE THEM STAND UP.

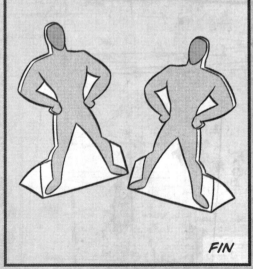

FIN

NOW SCOOP UP YOUR ARMY OF VILLAINS AND TAKE THEM WITH YOU WHEREVER YOU GO!

137

YOU WOULD NOT WANT TO BE SPIDER-MAN. JUST *ASK* HIM, HE'LL TELL YOU. BUT SERIOUSLY, THIS GUY HAS BEEN FRIENDS WITH OR KNOWN SO MANY PEOPLE WHO TURNED OUT TO BE SUPER VILLAINS, IT'S NOT EVEN *FUNNY*. EXCEPT FOR THE PART ABOUT IT BEING PRETTY FUNNY. THAT PART'S *HILARIOUS*.

IT'S A BUMMER WHEN MOST OF THE PEOPLE YOU KNOW ARE REALLY BAD GUYS

GREEN-GOBLIN

WHO HE IS: Norman Osborn

OCCUPATION: Businessman, stealer of other people's ideas

GREEN-GOBLIN

WHO HE IS: Harry Osborn (Norman's son)

OCCUPATION: Took over "family business" from dad

HOBGOBLIN

WHO HE IS: Roderick Kingsley

OCCUPATION: Millionaire fashion designer

ROB-GOBLIN

WHO HE IS: Just kidding, there is no Rob Goblin.

J. JONAH JAMESON

WHO HE IS: Uh, J. Jonah Jameson? We just said it.

OCCUPATION: Publisher of *Daily Bugle*, guy who funded creation of the Scorpion and the Spider-Slayers

SEE IF YOU CAN MATCH THE VILLAIN WITH HIS OR HER SECRET IDENTITY! *GOOD LUCK*, YOU'RE GONNA NEED IT. THIS ONE IS SO TOUGH, EVEN TONY STARK (A VERY SMART MAN) *COULDN'T* FIGURE IT OUT! WE HOPE YOU PUT ON YOUR *SMARTY* PANTS, YOUR *SMARTY* SHIRT, *AND* YOUR *SMARTY* SHOES (SMARTY SOCKS *OPTIONAL*, AND WE ASSUME YOU'RE ALREADY WEARING SMARTY *UNDERWEAR*).

WHO'S WHO?

VILLAIN

A. ANVIL

B. AWESOME ANDROID

C. BASILISK

D. BIRD-MAN

E. BROTHERS GRIMM

F. KLAW

G. KRAVEN THE HUNTER

H. THE OWL

I. POUNDCAKES

J. PROFESSOR POWER

K. ZARRKO THE TOMORROW MAN

SECRET IDENTITY

1. JOHNNY ANVIL

2. AWESOME ANDROID

3. BASIL ELKS

4. HENRY HAWK

5. PERCY AND BARTON GRIMES

6. ULYSSES KLAW

7. SERGEI KRAVINOFF

8. LELAND OWLSLEY

9. MARIAN POUNCY

10. PROFESSOR ANTHONY POWER

11. ARTUR ZARRKO

ANSWERS:

A. 1, B. 2, C. 3, D. 4, E. 5 . . . You get the idea, right? It's not like there was any point in mixing them up.

DID YOU KNOW?

ARNOLD PAFFENROTH IS SECRETLY THE VILLAINOUS *TATTERDEMALION*? WE DIDN'T EITHER.

There's an old saying: "Sometimes *less* is more." Usually, that's true, like when you have to spend time with your weird relative who collects statues of cats dressed as cowboys (wait, that's *our* weird relative). But sometimes *more* is more! Like when you want to talk, talk, talk to make super villains lose their minds. We've compiled some of the best things you can say that are guaranteed to do just that.

DRIVE THE BAD GUYS NUTS JUST BY TALKING

SAY THIS "HEY, DID YOU WIN THAT SILLY-LOOKING SUIT IN A CONTEST, OR WERE YOU THE LOSER?"

SAY THIS "YOU REMIND ME OF SOMEONE I KNOW, BUT UGLIER AND MEANER AND MORE SUPER VILLAINY. BUT THE ANNOYING LAUGH AND CONSTANT NEED TO REMIND ME THAT YOU'RE GOING TO TAKE OVER THE WORLD ARE THE SAME."

SAY THIS "I WOULD CALL YOU A DOOFUS, BUT THAT WOULD BE AN INSULT TO ALL THE OTHER DOOFUSES. OR IS IT 'DOOFI'? I ALWAYS GET THE PLURAL CONFUSED."

SAY THIS "ALL THE OTHER SUPER VILLAINS TOOK A POLL TO DECIDE WHO'S THE SMELLIEST. CONGRATULATIONS, YOU TOPPED THE LIST!"

SAY THIS "ON THE WHOLE, I'D RATHER BE FIGHTING THE GIBBON."

ARE YOU *SURE* THIS BOOK ISN'T CALLED "LET'S MAKE FUN OF THE *GIBBON*"?

WE'LL KEEP HARPING ON THIS: YOU *HAVE* TO KNOW THE BAD GUYS! WHEN YOU'RE OUT IN THE FIELD, YOU MAY CATCH JUST A FLEETING *GLIMPSE* OF AN ARM OR A LEG. YOU'LL HAVE TO BE ABLE TO IDENTIFY THE THREAT ON THE *SPOT!* SEE HOW YOU DO WITH OUR TRICKY TEST.

VILLAIN IDENTIFICATION

WHAT YOU NEED TO DO:

1. Take a **look** at the boxes.

2. See if you can identify each **bad guy** represented by the figure.

3. **Check** your answers below.

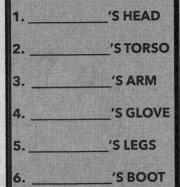

ANSWERS:

1. _____'S HEAD

2. _____'S TORSO

3. _____'S ARM

4. _____'S GLOVE

5. _____'S LEGS

6. _____'S BOOT

YOU KNOW 'EM, YOU LOVE 'EM, YOU CAN'T LIVE WITHOUT 'EM. WE'RE NOT TALKING ABOUT YOUR WEIRD RELATIVE WHO COLLECTS STATUES OF CATS DRESSED AS COWBOYS—*AGAIN*, THAT'S OUR WEIRD RELATIVE. *NO*, WE'RE TALKING ABOUT *BAD GUYS*. IT'S TIME TO PICK YOUR *ENEMIES!*

MENACING, UH, MENACES!

HERE'S WHAT YOU DO: *GET* THE ATTRIBUTE AND NUMBER DICE. GET THEM *NOW!* *ROLL* THE DICE, MAKING NOTE OF THE ICON AND NUMBER THAT COME UP. FIND THEM IN THE CHART ON PAGE 143. YOU CAN PICK ONE ENEMY FOR EACH ICON AND NUMBER YOU ROLLED. IF YOU ROLLED A 6 OR A 1, YOU CAN PICK ONE MORE ENEMY FROM ANYWHERE ON THE PAGE!

IF THERE'S A VILLAIN YOU REALLY, *REALLY* WANT TO HAVE AS AN ENEMY (AND *WHY* WOULD YOU WANT THAT?), YOU CAN WRITE YOUR *OWN* IN THE *BLANKS* PROVIDED.

① ATTRIBUTES!

1. INTELLIGENCE

KANG
A.I.M.

_____

2. STRENGTH

GREEN GOBLIN
TITANIUM MAN

_____

3. SPEED

RED SKULL
THE U-FOES

_____

4. DURABILITY

M.O.D.O.K.
CROSSBONES

_____

5. ENERGY PROJECTION

LOKI
CRIMSON DYNAMO

_____

6. FIGHTING

THE LEADER
DRACULA

_____

② SPECIAL POWERS!

BARON STRUCKER
THE GIBBON

_____

THANOS
ZARRKO THE
TOMORROW MAN

_____

RONAN
TOAD MEN

_____

DOCTOR OCTOPUS
IRON MONGER

_____

ABOMINATION
MALEKITH

_____

HYDRA
CHAMELEON

_____

143

LET'S SEE IF YOU WERE PAYING *ATTENTION*. ANSWER THESE QUESTIONS, AND IF YOU GET THEM ALL RIGHT, MAYBE—JUST *MAYBE*— THE GREEN GOBLIN WON'T PAY YOU A VISIT. BUT IF HE *DOES*, REMEMBER THAT GREEN IS HIS *FAVORITE* COLOR AND HE LIKES *BROWNIES* AND HE *HATES* SPIDER-MAN, SO DON'T BRING HIM UP.

TERRIBLE TEST

1 What can you build with macaroni and glue?

→ **A PIONEER CABIN** OR **A LIFE-SIZE STATUE OF M.O.D.O.K.**

2 Which Super Villain has photographic reflexes?

→ **TASKMASTER** OR **PHOTO REFLEXO, THE MADE-UP MAN**

3 What was Black Widow before she joined the Avengers?

→ **REALITY SHOW CONTESTANT** OR **SPY**

4 Why do we make so much fun of the Gibbon in this book?

→ **IT'S PRETTY OBVIOUS, RIGHT?** OR **WE DON'T MAKE FUN OF HIM SO MUCH AS USE GENTLE HUMOR TO POINT OUT THE SILLINESS OF . . . NO, WE MAKE FUN OF HIM.**

5 If you were a millionaire fashion designer, you would secretly be:

→ **THE HOBGOBLIN** OR **ROB GOBLIN**

ALL RIGHT, *TRUE BELIEVER!* THIS IS WHAT YOU'VE BEEN *WAITING* FOR.

AFTER THAT, IT'S BEEN ABOUT YOUR TRAINING TO BECOME THE *ULTIMATE* SUPER HERO.

THIS *ENTIRE* BOOK HAS BEEN ABOUT *ONE* THING AND *ONE* THING ONLY—MAKING *FUN* OF THE GIBBON.

REMEMBER *EVERYTHING* YOU LEARNED . . .

AND EVERYTHING YOU DIDN'T*!*

ASTONISHING ADVENTURES!

CHAPTER EIGHT

HOW TO PLAY:

YOU'LL NEED THE *ATTRIBUTE* AND *NUMBER* DICE, ALONG WITH YOUR COMPLETED MARVEL UNIVERSE *PROFILE.*

FOLLOW THE INSTRUCTIONS ON EACH PAGE.

OTHER TIMES, YOU'LL HAVE TO *ADD* THE NUMBER YOU ROLLED TO ONE OF YOUR ATTRIBUTES (*INTELLIGENCE, STRENGTH, SPEED, DURABILITY, ENERGY PROJECTION, FIGHTING*) AND TURN TO A CERTAIN PAGE.

ALONG THE WAY, YOU'LL BE ASKED TO *ROLL* THE DICE. SOMETIMES YOU'LL BE ASKED TO *TURN* TO A PAGE.

THE ONE THING YOU *WON'T* DO IS READ ALL OF THESE PAGES IN ORDER, BECAUSE IT WILL NOT MAKE ANY SENSE.

UNLESS YOU LIKE THINGS THAT *DON'T* MAKE SENSE. IN WHICH CASE, *HAPPY* READING!

FINAL

DAILY BUGLE

THE PICTURE NEWSPAPER®

New York, Saturday, Sept. 12, 1981

25¢

Sunny. High in the 70s.

Circulation: Five million

Ferdinand Torres

(Your name here, nice and big! You've made the front page!)

THREAT OR MENACE!

What a day. You were late to school, missed lunch, and have a stack of homework that makes the Hulk look short. Then you see the latest news. The *Daily Bugle* called you a menace. Can you believe it? You, a rookie Super Hero! You haven't even had a chance to become misunderstood like Spider-Man, and already they're calling you a menace. Sheesh.

On your way home from school, you get off the subway train and climb up the stairs to the busy New York City streets. Suddenly, you hear a bank alarm! How do you know it's a bank alarm? That's not important right now!* You know something's not right. What do you do?

ROLL YOUR NUMBER DICE!

If you roll **1**, **3**, or **5**: You head off in search of the alarm. Turn to page **157**.

If you roll **2**, **4**, or **6**: You think the alarm might be a diversion. Turn to page **147**.

146

*You clearly have a power we didn't tell you about: bank-alarm sense. It's like spider-sense, but for bank alarms.

*C*hanging into your costume, you forgo the bank alarm. It's too obvious, and you're pretty sure that someone's up to something a lot more sinister than getting rich. Running along a rooftop, you hear what sounds like the high-pitched hiss of a firework. Suddenly, a pumpkin explodes right before your eyes!

"THE GREEN GOBLIN!" you say, ducking the explosion. As if on cue, you see the Green Goblin flying on his goblin glider. He's digging into his bag of tricks. He pulls something from the bag and throws it at you.

"What's the matter, hero?" cackles the Goblin. "Got your ghost?"

ROLL YOUR NUMBER DICE!

If you roll a **2**, **3**, **4**, **5**, or **6**, turn to page **150**.

If you roll a **1**, turn to page **151**.

"*I* may be a rookie Super Hero," you say, "but I know that it's not every day you see dinosaurs running around New York City."

As the police do their best to get people to safety, you use your powers to keep the dinosaurs at bay. Your keen mind quickly takes note that you're dealing with a *Tyrannosaurus rex* and two velociraptors. You've had better days. Each dinosaur seems to have a metal band, flashing purple, around its arm.

These dinos must be rich to afford fancy jewelry like that! you think as you dodge a razor-toothed velociraptor.

That "fancy jewelry" tells you that someone is behind this stunt. But before you can do anything about it, you're face to face with an angry—and hungry—*T. rex*!

ROLL YOUR NUMBER DICE!

ADD THAT NUMBER TO YOUR FIGHTING SCORE.

If you got **8** or more: Your punch sure packs a wallop! Turn to page **152**.

If you got **4** or less: You're smacked by the *T. rex*'s tail! You're down for the count. Turn to page **153**.

If you got **5**, **6**, or **7**: The *T. rex* doesn't even seem to notice you! Turn to page **154**.

"**S**urprised to see me, hero?" someone screams from behind the dinosaurs.

You whip your head around and spot a tall man wearing what looks like a gorilla suit.

"Gorilla Man? Major Monkey?" you ask, honestly trying to figure out who's talking to you.

"The Gibbon! I'm the Gibbon!" the man shouts. "And the Gibbon spells . . . **doom**!"

"Actually, **D-O-O-M** spells 'doom,'" you answer. "You're not gonna pass a spelling test any time soon."

Frustrated and furious, the Gibbon leaps toward you.

ROLL YOUR ATTRIBUTE DICE!

If you roll **Strength**, **Speed**, **Durability**, **Energy Projection**, or **Fighting**, you evade the Gibbon's attack. This was clearly a false alarm, and you take on the dinosaurs. Turn to page **148**.

If you roll **Intelligence**, you succumb to the Gibbon's attack, which is embarrassing. Turn to page **146** and try again!

You can't believe your bad luck! A perfectly boring day has been ruined by the surprise appearance of the Green Goblin! He's thrown something at you, and as it gets closer, you can see what it is . . . a translucent ghost that slowly begins to grow!

You've got just one chance to avoid certain danger, hero.

 ROLL YOUR NUMBER DICE!

ADD THAT NUMBER TO YOUR SPEED SCORE.

If you have a score of **4** or less, turn to page **156**.

If you have a score of **5** or **6**, turn to page **155**.

If you have a score greater than **6**, turn to page **154**.

"**D**id you just throw a little ghost at me? Who does that?" you say as you easily dodge the Goblin's weapon. The ghost hits a nearby water tower and explodes. The impact knocks the Goblin off his glider, and the two of you are now standing face to face on the rooftop.

"Say good-bye, hero," says the Goblin. He points a finger at you, and you hear the hum of energy. He's getting ready to finish you off with his Goblin Blast!

ROLL YOUR NUMBER DICE!

If you roll a **1**, **2**, **3**, **4**, or **5**, it's all over. The Goblin unleashes a Goblin Blast that knocks you out. When you wake up, the Green Goblin is long gone. Looks like this is . . .

THE END!

If you roll a **6**, turn to page **161**.

*T*he crowd goes wild as your power-packed punch takes the *T. rex* down! You look at your fist, then glance at the dinosaur lying on the pavement before you. Not bad for a rookie Super Hero! But there's no time to savor this victory. You've got two more dinosaurs to deal with! Or . . . do you?

You notice the metal bands on each dinosaur begin to glow purple and flash faster and faster. Quicker than you can say "Go to jail, Gibbon," the dinosaurs disappear.

"Good job, son!" comes a voice from behind you. You turn to see Captain America—*the* Captain America—right in front of you! "I got here as soon as I could, but it looks like you've already taken care of the problem!"

You tell Cap everything that happened, especially about the metal bands and the flashing purple lights.

ROLL YOUR ATTRIBUTE DICE!

If you roll **Intelligence**, **Speed**, or **Energy Projection**: You managed to snag one of the metal bands before the dinosaurs disappeared. Turn to page **160**.

If you roll **Strength**, **Durability**, or **Fighting**: You didn't get one of the metal bands. Turn to page **164**.

"Oh, man," you say as you wake up, rubbing your aching head. "Did somebody get the number of that dinosaur?"

"Right now it is not dinosaurs that need concern you," comes a low voice. "You are unfamiliar to me, hero. No matter, you will suffer the fate of all heroes."

Slowly rising to your feet, you find yourself inside what appears to be a high-tech holding cell. A prison. There are no bars, but it doesn't take a genius like Tony Stark to figure out there's some kind of energy field keeping you in.

"But before that, you will tell me everything you know." You see several people wearing yellow suits and what look like beekeeper helmets. You'd laugh at the sight, but floating right beside them is a man in a hover chair. A man with an enormous head.

M.O.D.O.K.

THE END!

Your adventure is over . . . unless you turn to page **146** and try again!

"**H**ello, is anyone at home?" you hear someone yell, and you snap your head up from your desk, wiping a thin stream of drool from your mouth.

You could have sworn you were fighting dinosaurs, or maybe it was the Green Goblin . . . or who knows what. But that's not what happened at all! Those long hours of school and Super Hero-ing have taken their toll, and you tried to take a nap in Mr. Warren's science class!

"Do try to stay awake, class," says Mr. Warren.

"*Pssst!* That must have been some dream, huh?" says the student to your left. "Don't worry, you wouldn't believe the crazy, uh, dreams I have. Let me know if you need any help with your homework later!"

That Peter Parker's a pretty nice guy, you think. You're grateful that you're not caught up in some crazy Super Villain battle, but you'd be a little more grateful if you could go home and go to sleep!

THE END!

Your adventure is over . . . unless you turn to page **146** and try again!

"Impossible! I've never seen such speed!" says the Green Goblin as you manage to evade his grinning ghost. "Only Spider-Man can move that fast!"

You take advantage of the Goblin's surprise to use your powers. Landing a blow, you knock the Goblin from his glider, which smashes into a nearby chimney! The explosion sends bricks flying.

"Looks like it's just you and me, Gobby!" you say to your purple-and-green foe. "Now suppose you tell me what you're up to like a nice little Goblin, and then I'll take you to jail."

The Goblin chuckles as he slowly rises to his feet. He stands before a nearby water tower. "Enjoy my Goblin Blast, hero!" With that, the Super Villain unleashes an electric burst from his outstretched finger!

 **ROLL YOUR NUMBER DICE!**

ADD THAT NUMBER TO YOUR INTELLIGENCE SCORE.

If you have **5** or more, turn to page **161**.

If you have **4** or less, turn to page **162**.

You're fast, but unfortunately, you aren't fast enough this time. The ghost grows and grows at an exponential rate and soon envelopes you. You're now trapped inside the Green Goblin's gruesome ghost!

"So much for you, Super Hero!" snarls the Green Goblin. He laughs as you struggle against the ghostly prison. No matter how hard you punch or how you use your powers, nothing seems to puncture the ghost. It's like it's made of steel!

"Aren't you supposed to, like, pick on Spider-Man and stuff?" you ask.

"Yeah, aren't you supposed to, like, pick on Spider-Man and stuff?" someone echoes.

The Goblin turns around, surprised, only to be greeted by Spider-Man's feet slamming into his stomach! Tumbling off his glider, the Goblin lands on the rooftop in a daze.

Spider-Man lands in a crouching position and uses his spectacular spider strength to tear open the ghost.

"Leave the Super Hero-ing to the professionals, rookie!" says Spidey. For now, this is . . .

THE END!

Your adventure is over . . . unless you turn to page **146** and try again!

*Y*ou race through the busy streets of New York's Times Square, shoving through the crowd with murmurs of "Excuse me!" and "Sorry!" Running into an empty alley,* you make the switch from your everyday street clothes into your Super Hero guise. The kids at school would freak if they knew you were secretly some kind of super-powered adventurer!

It takes only seconds, but now you're hitting the streets as a full-fledged rookie Super Hero. The crowds of people point at you with excitement. They can't believe it's you! There's no time to waste, so you jump into action, taking off in the direction of the bank alarm. Rounding the corner, you see the trouble—a trio of dinosaurs has smashed the bank to rubble! And not just the bank, but other buildings, too, and—wait, **DINOSAURS?**

ROLL YOUR NUMBER DICE!

If you roll **1**, **2**, **3**, **4**, or **6**: You leap into action to stop the dinosaurs. Turn to page **148**.

If you roll **5**: You see something lurking behind the dinosaurs. Turn to page **149**.

*See page 110.

Before Kang can even move, you use your powers to rupture the Conqueror's strange weapon. As a glowing purple energy pours forth, you see Kang begin to panic.

"No, no!" he says. "Not when I was so close! I will not be denied my revenge against the Avengers! Noooooooo!!!!"

There's a brilliant burst of purple light. As quickly as they appeared, Kang and his dinosaur army vanish.

"Well done, hero!" says Captain America. He revs up his motorcycle and turns back toward New York City. "If you ever need help, you know who to call. The Avengers owe you one!"

You can't believe your luck. Not only did you team up with the first Avenger, Captain America, but you faced –and defeated–Kang! Way to go!

Now if only Cap hadn't left you stranded in the middle of the George Washington Bridge . . .

*Y*ou leap off of Captain America's motorcycle, throwing yourself right against one of Kang's dinosaur minions. WHAM! Your strength, coupled with your momentum, knocks the time-lost beast to the side. You're now standing face to face with Kang the Conqueror!

"Sorry, Kang, but this is going to hurt you a lot more than it's going to hurt me," you say. As you get ready to use your powers, Kang touches a button on his belt. His suit begins to radiate waves of energy that send you reeling backward!

"You may not touch me, hero!" bellows Kang. He aims that strange weapon at you, enveloping you in a burst of purple. "I will have my revenge against the Avengers. And *you* will spend the rest of your life in Earth's Jurassic era!"

As the purple light dissolves, you blink. Where once you stood on the George Washington Bridge, now you stand in what looks like a tropical paradise. A pteranodon soars overhead, and you see a brachiosaur nibbling on some leaves.

"Okay, I got this," you say. "And when I get back, Kang better watch out!"

THE END!

Your adventure is over . . . unless you turn to page **146** and try again!

"I hope you don't mind my tagging along," says Captain America. "Looks like you could use a hand."

Wow! A chance to team up with an Avenger, and it's Captain America to boot! How cool is that? If you had your phone, you would take a selfie so fast it would make Quicksilver look like your Uncle Vern after Thanksgiving dinner.*

Focus, hero, focus!

"I sure could use the help, Cap!" you say. You hop on the back of Cap's motorcycle, and the two of you head toward the George Washington Bridge into New Jersey. "I've got a hunch," you say to Cap. "All we have to do is track the source of the signals coming from this band I swiped from a dinosaur!"

ROLL YOUR NUMBER DICE!

If you roll a **1**, **3**, or **5**: Cap follows your hunch. Turn to page **163**.

If you roll a **2**, **4**, or **6**: Uh-oh. Turn to page **164**.

*Uncle Vern moves so very, very slowly after eating Thanksgiving dinner.

*T*he Green Goblin may be pretty smart, but you're just a little smarter! Using your powers, you rip open the water tower near the Goblin. As water rushes out, it douses the Super Villain—causing his Goblin Blast to short out!

"Curse you, hero!" hisses the Goblin, as he's knocked unconscious by your quick thinking.

Seconds later, you hear the sound of something whooshing through the air. Swinging in for a landing via an impossibly thin strand of webbing is the amazing Spider-Man!

"Hey, thanks, kid!" says Spidey. "I've been tracking the Goblin all over town. Wanna help me take this goofball to the police station?"

Help Spider-Man? How cool is that! Not a bad day for a rookie Super Hero!

THE END!
WAY TO GO!

*J*ust as the Goblin Blast hits you full force, you think, *I should have smashed open that water tower. . . . I bet the water could have short-circuited the Goblin's powers!* But it's too late for that, and as you slowly fall unconscious, you see the gloating Goblin standing over you.

"You'll make wonderful bait for Spider-Man," he says. "Go to sleep, little Super Hero. Soon Spider-Man will be no more, and it's all thanks to you!"

Your adventure is over . . . unless you turn to page **146** and try again!

As you and Cap zoom across the George Washington Bridge, a bright flash of purple light appears just above the road in front of you. Suddenly, you see the dinosaurs from before blocking your path. Only this time they've brought a friend. . . .

"Kang!" you shout. It's the Avengers' archfoe, the self-proclaimed Conqueror and master of time.

As he levels a strange-looking device at you and Captain America, Kang speaks. "I see the Avengers have chosen a new ally. A pity I will have to send you both back into Earth's distant past, never to return!"

ROLL YOUR ATTRIBUTE DICE!

If you roll **Intelligence**, **Speed**, or **Energy Projection**: You use your powers to target Kang's weapon. Turn to page **158**.

If you roll **Strength**, **Durability,** or **Fighting**: You leap directly at Kang. Turn to page **159**.

Before you can act on your hunch, you witness an incredible flare of purple energy that seems to engulf you and Captain America. You can't see anything now except for that purple light. Soon enough, it begins to fade. . . .

"Uh, Cap?" you say to the shield slinger. "Does this look like the George Washington Bridge to you?"

"No," says Cap. "No, it doesn't."

And with good reason. Where once you stood on a modern suspension bridge, you now find yourself in a patch of thick vegetation and trees. A screeching sound directs your attention to the skies above, where you see a . . . pteranodon?

"Kang," says Captain America. "He's the master of time. He must have sent us back here, hoping to keep us from stopping him."

"Well, it won't work!" you shout. "Uh, right, Cap?"

"No, it won't! There's always a way, hero. And we'll find it!"

THE END!

Your adventure is over . . . unless you turn to page **146** and try again!

MARVEL UNIVERSE CHARACTER SHEET CHECKLIST

HERO NAME:
Chapter 3

REAL NAME:
Chapter 1

IDENTITY:
Chapter 1

POWERS:
Chapter 2

SPECIAL SKILLS AND ABILITIES:
Chapter 5

POWER GRID	1	2	3	4	5	6	7
INTELLIGENCE							
STRENGTH							
SPEED							
DURABILITY							
ENERGY PROJECTION							
FIGHTING							

OCCUPATION:
Chapter 1

Lawyer

ORIGIN:
Chapter 1

REASON YOU FIGHT CRIME:
Chapter 1

To help the lowly and the weak

BASE OF OPERATIONS:
Chapter 4

Secret lab underneath a shack

ALLIES:
Chapter 6

ENEMIES:
Chapter 7

DRAW YOUR SUPER HERO

COSTUME'S SPECIAL FEATURE:
Page 52

MY ULTIMATE SUPER HERO MANUAL INDEX

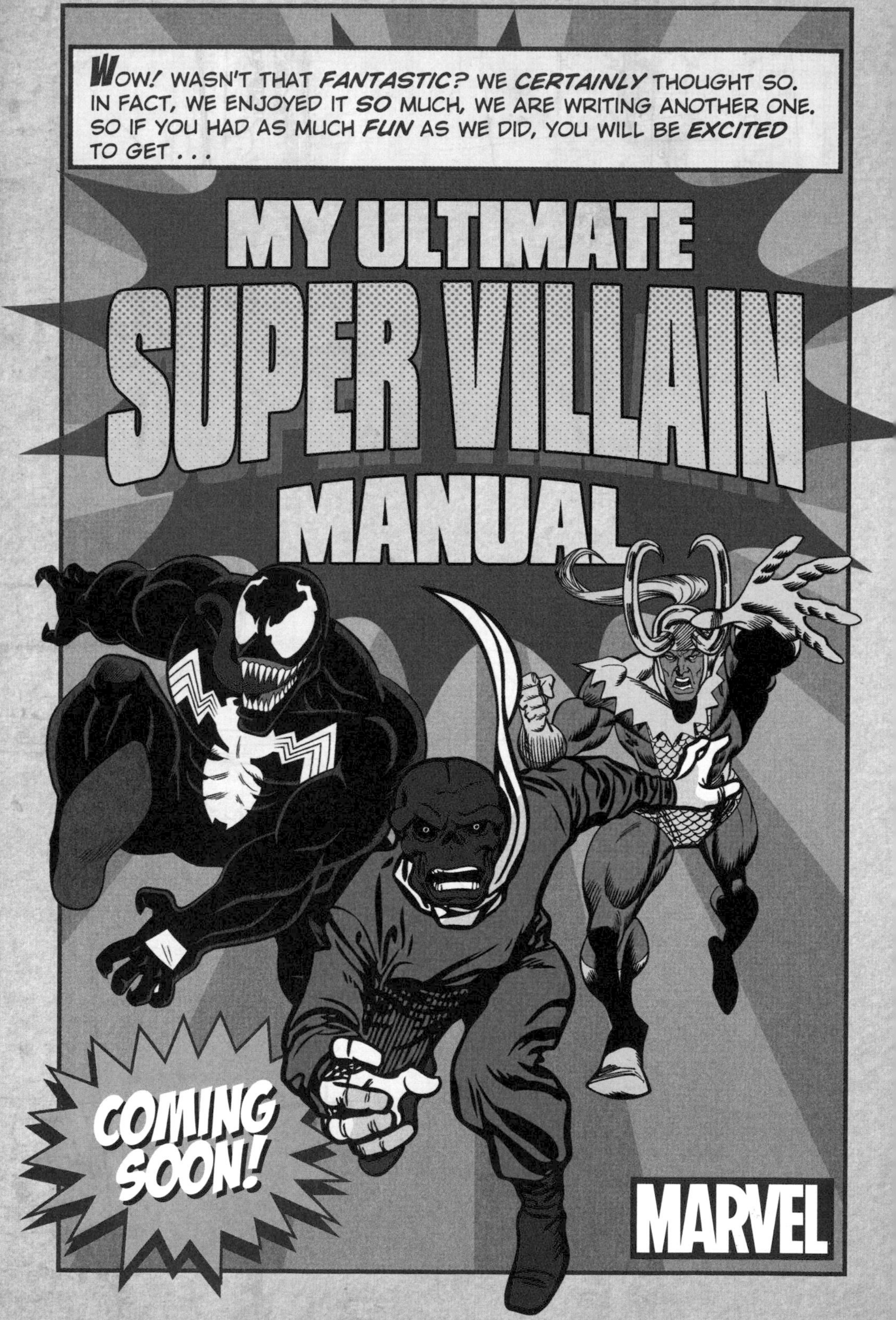
WOW! WASN'T THAT FANTASTIC? WE CERTAINLY THOUGHT SO. IN FACT, WE ENJOYED IT SO MUCH, WE ARE WRITING ANOTHER ONE. SO IF YOU HAD AS MUCH FUN AS WE DID, YOU WILL BE EXCITED TO GET . . .
MY ULTIMATE SUPER VILLAIN MANUAL
COMING SOON!
MARVEL